Knocking
New Beginnings Book 1
ROBIN MERRILL

Behold, I stand at the door and knock: if any man hear my voice and open the door, I will come in to him, and will sup with him, and he with me. —Revelation 3:20

Chapter 1

Esther

It felt like a kick to the stomach. Esther stopped breathing. She must have heard wrong. She looked around the sanctuary, trying to gauge the reactions of her friends. They looked shocked. Confused. Maybe she had heard correctly.

She returned her eyes to her pastor, but he was expressionless. "I'm sorry about this, ladies," he said. But he didn't sound sorry. He sounded ready for retirement.

Hot tears filled her eyes, and she let them spill down her cheek. Her arms felt too heavy to reach for a tissue.

"Let's stand for one more song together," he said and opened his hymnal.

Esther glanced around again and then followed suit. What else was there to do? Have an emotional outburst? Stomp out of the church in protest? No. She would sing a song with her sisters. Apparently, for the last time.

"Number two thirty-three," the pastor said, and the organist started to play. Instantly, Esther recognized the familiar notes, even before she saw the hymnal page.

She tried to sing past the lump in her throat, but she was singing a lie. It was *not* well with her soul. How could God do this? How could he rip her church away from her? This was all she had left! These were her friends. This was her one outing per week. This was her one source of comfort. This was what she looked forward to.

She thought of Russell, and the lump grew too big to sing around. She closed her mouth and silently wept. She'd married him in this sanctuary so many years ago. Their babies had been christened in this sanctuary. And then all their friends and family had said goodbye to Russell in this sanctuary. She looked at the light filtering through the stained-glass window. What would become of those windows? What would become of the building? She looked up at the rafters and breathed in the familiar scent of the place. She squeezed her eyes shut and prayed. "Change this. Fix this. Make this better. Don't let this happen to us." She opened her eyes, but nothing had changed. She looked over at Vicky. Vicky wasn't singing either. Vicky *always* sang. She'd been the star of the choir, back when they'd had a choir. Now she just stood there, leaning on the pew in front of her, looking shell-shocked. She hadn't been married in this church, but her kids had grown up there too. How many Christmas plays and Easter musicals had Vicky and she sat through? How many angel and shepherd costumes had they sewn together?

Vicky caught her staring, and Esther smiled, trying to be encouraging. Vicky did not return the smile. Instead, she returned her eyes to the pastor, and Esther realized something. Vicky was *angry*. And it was contagious. Esther realized she was angry too: with the pastor, though there was probably nothing he could have done; with the diocese; and, she realized, with God. Her eyes returned to the rafters. Being mad at God made her feel guilty, but didn't he deserve a little of her wrath right now? How could he do this to her? She'd served him since she was a child, and now, in her final years of life, he was going to take away her entire support system?

Her children lived halfway across the country. They were busy with their own lives, their own families. She didn't want to be a burden for them. The church was supposed to take care of the widows, and this is what they decided? To throw her out into the street? Who would help her when she needed it? Who would check on her when she was ill? Who would notice when she was missing? Who would notice when she was *gone?* Where would her funeral be held?

The song ended, and the pastor gave a benediction. Immediately, he was swarmed. "What are we supposed to do?" Barbara asked.

He put a hand on her shoulder. "If I were you, I would find another church. St. Thomas is nice."

"St. Thomas is *not* nice," she snapped, and Esther bit back a laugh. "I don't *want* another church. I want *my* church. Why didn't they give us any warning? We could have stopped this—"

The pastor held up a hand. "Ladies, there are seven of you. That's it. That is not enough to keep a church going. If you don't want to try St. Thomas, I recommend Calvary."

"Calvary?" Barbara cried. "In Belfast?" That was an hour away. None of them would be driving that far to attend church. None of them could afford to.

"That's the closest church that is within our diocese," he tried.

Vicky went after him then, asking what they could do to stop it.

Esther waited for that argument to play out and then asked, "What will happen to the building?"

"I'm sorry," the pastor said, cupping a hand over his ear. "What did you say, Esther?"

She tried to speak up. "What will happen to this building?"

He shrugged. "Nothing, for now. It will be vacant."

Chapter 2

Emma

"Dare you to knock on her door." Isabelle elbowed Emma in the side hard enough to hurt, and cherry slushy dripped off the end of Isabelle's straw and onto Emma's toe.

Emma stopped walking and shook her foot, but the slushy was like glue. Gross red glue. "Yuck, Isabelle! You don't need to whip your straw around spraying cherry syrup everywhere!"

The other three girls stopped walking too.

"Oh, relax, Miss Drama Queen," Isabelle said. "It's not like you can't take a shower. And stop dodging the dare."

"I'm not dodging the dare." Emma started walking again.

Isabelle didn't follow. She just stood there in the street, holding her stupid slushy in one hand and chewing on her straw. "Oh, you're not, are you?"

Emma didn't turn around.

"Prove it."

Finally, Emma turned and looked at her friends. "Don't be stupid. That's a stupid dare, and I'm not doing it. You're all acting like little kids." She turned away and started walking again.

"Chicken!" Natalie called after her.

Why were her friends siding with Isabelle again? This was so stupid. She didn't know what to do. She certainly wasn't going to go knock on Mrs. Patterson's door, no matter what. That would be embarrassing, not to mention kind of mean to Mrs. Patterson. But neither did Emma want to walk around town alone. That gave her the creeps, and someone was sure to tell her dad, and she would get in trouble. But going home was her *last* choice. Both of her parents were always exhausted after church, and they were probably napping or watching separate televisions—either way, they'd want her to be *quiet* so they could "rest."

She hated Sundays.

Trying to be firm, she continued walking, not knowing where she was going. Eventually, her friends gave up and caught up to her. Breath rushed out of her.

"I don't know why you don't want to do it," Isabelle said.

"I don't know why you want me to," Emma fired back.

"Because it would be hilarious," Raven chimed in.

"No, it wouldn't be. Where are we going, anyway? Let's go to the boat landing."

"Okay, let's," Isabelle said, and skipped ahead. Then she turned to face them. "Why are you so scared of your neighbor?"

"I'm not *scared* of her," Emma said, though this wasn't entirely true. "She's a sad old lady. I don't want to make her sadder by messing with her."

"Have you ever seen her?" Natalie asked.

No, she hadn't, but she didn't want to tell them that and deepen the intrigue.

"I wonder what she looks like," Isabelle said. "Maybe she's a hunchback or something. I don't know anyone who has seen her. You should knock on the door, and then when she comes to answer it, take her picture and then run away. Then you could show everyone what she looks like!"

Emma rolled her eyes. "Your ideas keep getting worse."

"*No*, they keep getting *better*."

"I'll do it!" Raven suddenly declared.

Emma's stomach rolled. She couldn't have any part of this. Her father would kill her.

Isabelle and Natalie stopped walking. "You *will*?" Isabelle said slowly, emphasizing her doubt.

Emma was surprised too. Raven was usually the last person to accept a dare.

"All I have to do is take her picture and run away, right?" She was already having second thoughts.

Isabelle put her arm around her. "Right. We'll be waiting in Emma's backyard. Run right for us, and then we'll all run to the boat landing."

"Okay," Raven said tentatively. She started to slide the phone out of her back pocket.

"Here," Isabelle said, shoving her phone in her face, "use mine."

"Why?"

"It's better."

Though Isabelle's phone *was* better, or at least miles more expensive, Emma knew that wasn't why she was pushing it into Raven's face. They had to use *her* phone so that she could show the picture to anyone and everyone who would look, and then take credit for the prank. Emma didn't want to be friends with Isabelle anymore, but it was so hard to avoid her. Isabelle was everywhere—even in church.

They started walking toward Mrs. Patterson's house, and Emma tried to think of a way to stop this. "I don't think this is a good idea." She hated how wobbly and weak her voice sounded.

"*Obviously*," Isabelle said, "and *obviously* you are wrong, and it is a *very* good idea."

Though it was the middle of the afternoon and the sun was high and bright in the sky, Isabelle made a show of slinking along the side of Emma's house to reach the backyard. Anyone driving by could see them. Mrs. Patterson, if she looked out her window, could see them. Isabelle went behind the grapevines and then pulled Natalie in with her. "Come on, hide!"

Raven ducked behind the vines too.

"Not you." Isabelle pushed her back out. "You've got a job to do."

Raven didn't move.

"You don't have to do this," Emma said.

"*Yes*, she does. Stop trying to take away her fun. You're just jealous because you didn't dare to do it."

Emma rolled her eyes.

"What does she look like?" Raven asked. "Is she scary?" Raven was the youngest girl in their class and acted it.

"No, she's just an old woman, and we really shouldn't be picking on her."

Isabelle elbowed Emma again, even harder this time. Then she looked at Raven. "We don't *know* what she looks like. That's the whole point. Now *go*, or we give up on you."

Chapter 3

Tonya

From the upstairs bathroom window, Tonya had a clear view of her daughter's friend tiptoeing across their lawn. Tonya scanned the area. Why was Raven tiptoeing? She was in plain sight, yet she was acting as if she was trying to sneak up on someone. But who? There was no one there. And where were the other girls? She wasn't sure, hadn't been paying much attention, but she thought Raven had been with Emma when Emma had left the house with a gaggle of neighborhood girls.

She slid the window open to holler to Raven, but then she wondered if it was worth the energy of interfering. Maybe she should just let Raven be weird. Maybe they were playing a harmless game.

Then she heard a giggle from below. She couldn't see anyone else, but she recognized the giggle: Isabelle.

So this game, whatever it was, wasn't harmless. She opened her mouth to holler, but then thought better of it. Maybe she should catch them in the act. If she continued watching, and witnessed something wayward, she would finally have something to take to Isabelle's mother, the bane of her existence. Or *one of* the banes of her existence.

Isabelle was the only child of a perfect little family who lived in a perfect giant house and did perfect things. Her father had a perfect job. They drove a perfect SUV. They wore perfect clothes. They were perfect, perfect, perfect.

Isabelle was *not* perfect. She was the church brat, but somehow, Tonya was the only one who seemed to know it. Isabelle was always causing trouble, but never getting caught. She was a bully half the time and sticky sweet the other half. She would call Emma fat one Sunday and then invite her to an expensive water park the next. Tonya had tried to talk to Isabelle's mother about it, but she'd gotten nowhere. *No way* would Isabelle steal all the fish crackers out of the church nursery, or turn all the sound room dials up to max, or fling glow-in-the-dark paint all over the sanctuary carpet.

Too late, Tonya realized that Raven was approaching Mrs. Patterson's door. She hollered Raven's name, but the girl didn't hear her. Or at least she pretended she didn't. Tonya flew out of the bathroom, down the stairs, down the hallway, past her husband on the couch, and out the back door to find the other three girls crouching behind the grapevine. She ignored them for the moment and headed toward Raven, who was already knocking on Mrs. Patterson's door.

"Raven, stop!"

Raven heard her this time and looked at her. Then she looked past her, toward the grapevine.

The door opened.

"Come here, Raven," she said, trying to use her gentle pastor's wife voice. The fake one.

Raven looked at the open doorway, presumably at Mrs. Patterson, but Tonya couldn't see her. Then Raven looked at the grapevine. Then, much to Tonya's horror, she picked up her phone, flashed it in Mrs. Patterson's face, and took off running toward Tonya. Tonya hurried to Mrs. Patterson's door, but by the time she got there, it was closed again. She knocked, not expecting an answer. When they'd first moved in, she had tried to visit multiple times, to bring her a pie, to invite her to church, to sell Girl Scout cookies, and that door never opened.

It didn't open now either. Exhausted, Tonya leaned on the rickety porch railing. "Mrs. Patterson, I'm so sorry about that," she called out. "That was rude and awful, but I want you to know that I will deal with it." She paused. Was there anything else she could say? "You have a nice day," she said and then wished she hadn't. How could anyone who lived alone and never left their house have a nice day? She couldn't believe the woman had even opened the door for Raven.

Tonya backed away from the door and turned toward the grapevine. Of course, the girls weren't there anymore. She went back into the house, grabbed her car keys, and got behind the wheel. Emma was going to be grounded for a very long time.

Chapter 4

Esther

Esther was too upset to sit still. She'd tried to knit and watch television, but she couldn't stop thinking about her church, and the more she thought about it, the harder it was to sit still. She thought about eating something. She still hadn't had lunch. But she had no appetite. She decided to go for a walk. This was only a little unusual for her. Though her doctor had told her to walk every day, she managed it once a month. But today was a perfect, beautiful day, and so she decided a walk might calm her mind a bit.

She put on her sneakers and headed outside. She lived in an apartment building specifically for people like her. Mostly widows with a few spinsters mixed in. All on a fixed income. All lonely.

The sunshine felt good on her face and arms, and she breathed in the fresh air. On most July days, she wouldn't want to be outside walking in the summer heat, but today the temperature was perfect, and a breeze blew in off the sea.

Her building sat on a street corner, and she turned away from Main Street and headed down the smaller side street, Providence Ave. It was a small town, but Main Street was still too loud. It had been even worse back when the paper mill was open. Russell had worked at that paper mill for thirty-seven years. Then they'd shut it down, giving him about as much advanced notice as she'd had from the church. It wasn't a fond memory. They'd been scared. The economy hadn't been good, and he hadn't known how to do anything else. He only knew how to make paper.

But they'd made it work. He'd found a job at a lumberyard. He made a lot less there, but it was all right, as they didn't have any debt, and they didn't have expensive hobbies. She'd always loved the way he smelled when he came home from the lumberyard. Like pine.

She realized she was passing by an old church. She stopped and looked up at it. She'd driven and walked by this church countless times, but this was the first time in ages that she'd really looked at it. She tried to remember the last time it had been open. Sometime in the seventies, she thought. She shook her head. What a shame. A crooked for sale sign hung in the yard. That had been there for as long as she could remember. No one wanted to buy an old church. She stepped onto the lawn, which was long overdue for a mow. The place had been beautiful once. It was a wreck now. The stained-glass windows had been removed, and the holes boarded up. Paint flaked off the walls. The basement windows were broken, and someone had spray-painted graffiti on the walls. This looked particularly awful because there was no graffiti in Carver Harbor. Ever.

Was this what was going to happen to her church? Were they going to slap a for sale sign in front of it and then let it go to ruin? She didn't know if she could take that.

She heard a noise and looked up. A bird flew out from under the rafter. Good, at least someone was still being blessed by the place. She smiled.

A small group of giggling girls interrupted her reverie. She turned to watch them run down the street. They were beautiful. So young, so carefree, so energetic. She didn't know what they were laughing at, but something had sure struck them funny—or at least three of them were laughing. One of them looked sad and only seemed to be trying to catch up.

Esther smiled at the sad girl, but none of the girls saw her.

Then the loudest one flung a plastic slushy cup over her right shoulder, not even looking to see where it would land. It flew within feet of Esther and landed in the tall grass of the church's lawn.

Esther sighed. She went and picked the cup and the sticky straw out of the long grass. She gave the old church one last look. "I'm sorry this happened to you," she said quietly, "and to your people." Then she headed back to her apartment building so she could throw away the litter.

She'd been wrong. Her walk hadn't made her feel any better.

Chapter 5

Emma

Emma heard crunching gravel and knew it was her mother before she even saw the car. And though she knew she was about to get it, part of her was relieved that her mother was coming for her. She couldn't wait to climb into the safety of that old car.

"Uh-oh," Isabelle sang, "someone's in trouble." She didn't even try to hide her delight.

Raven looked scared.

"Look!" Isabelle held up her phone.

It took Emma a second to realize what she was looking at. Then, when she did, she felt sick.

Isabelle had posted the picture on social media.

"You didn't say you were going to do that!" Raven cried.

"I didn't say I wasn't, either." Looking down at her phone, Isabelle gave a smug smile that made Emma hate her. Really hate her.

"Emma! Get in the car!"

Emma headed that way before her mother finished her sentence. But even though Emma was obeying, her mother left the car and headed toward her—and then right past her.

Oh no. Please don't, Mom. They're not your kids.

"I am so disappointed in you young ladies. Why would you do something like that?"

Emma climbed into the car, slammed the door, and put her head in her hands.

"I will be discussing this with each of your parents."

Isabelle snickered, and Emma went from being embarrassed by her mother to worried about her. Her mother was sensitive and didn't have an easy life. She didn't need to be disrespected by the likes of Isabelle.

Emma started to climb back out of the car, but her mother had already turned and headed her way, her face twisted up in fury. Emma felt sick to her stomach.

Her mom slammed the door so hard that the whole car shook.

"I'm sorry," Emma said quietly.

"I'm sure you are." Her mother didn't believe her. She threw the car in drive and then peeled out, spraying gravel behind them. Her fingers clutched the steering wheel in a death grip.

"I tried to stop it."

"Well, you didn't try hard enough." There was a hardness in her mother's voice that she wasn't used to.

Emma felt horrible about what Isabelle and Raven—mostly Isabelle—had done, but was her mother overreacting? She didn't know what her mother wanted her to say, so she stayed quiet for a minute. Then she thought of something *she* wanted said. "Thank you for coming to get me."

Her mother's fingers relaxed their grip on the wheel, and she took a deep breath. "You know I love you, right?"

"Yes."

"Good. I will love you no matter what. You can't do anything to change that, ever. But I am really disappointed in you right now. I can't believe *my* daughter did something so cruel."

Yes, she was overreacting, and she didn't even know about the social media piece. "I'm sorry." A thought occurred to her. "Is this because I'm a pastor's kid?"

Her mother answered with a guttural, humorless laugh. "No, not at all."

This was a small comfort.

"I want you to grow up to be the strong, kind woman that I know you are. I know there will be missteps. I'm not asking you to be perfect, but I still have high expectations of you because I know you." She took a shaky breath. "I wish that being a pastor's kid didn't offer additional pressure. I'm sorry that it does, but that pressure will never come from me."

Emma had heard variations of this sentiment before, but it still felt good to hear it again. "Isabelle tried to make me do it, and I said no. But then she told Raven, and Raven didn't have the guts to say no. I didn't know how to stop it, Mom. I really didn't. If I could have thought of a way, I would have."

Her mom nodded. "I think you should go apologize to Mrs. Patterson. Invite Raven and Natalie to come along."

Emma's stomach rolled.

"You can invite Isabelle too, of course, but I'll eat my hat if she agrees."

"Mom, I don't think I can."

"Yes, you can. I'll go with you. And we should probably bring her a treat."

Of course. Her mother always tried to fix things with cookies and pie.

Chapter 6

Esther

E sther was disappointed with herself for how upset she was. Her mind tried to tell her that she was overreacting, but her emotions disagreed. She tried to watch television, but she kept right on crying. Her church. Her beloved church was gone. Her home was gone.

She made a TV dinner and ate it on the couch. When she'd finished, she wasn't quite full, so she made another.

Then, her stomach full and her heart broken, she lay down on the couch. Her eyelids grew heavy, and, still listening to the rerun, she drifted off to sleep.

She was in church, but it wasn't her church. When she realized that Russell was sitting beside her, fresh tears sprang to her eyes. She looked up at him and gasped—he looked thirty-five! He looked down at her and smiled, and then patted her knee. She looked down at his hand and saw her own legs. They were young too! She wrapped her hand around his and relished the warmth of it. Then she looked around the sanctuary. She didn't recognize it. They must be visiting a different church. But wow, wasn't it full! A large family sat in the pew in front of them. The father had his arm around the mother, and four little girls sat beside them. Only the one on the end fidgeted. The little girl caught Esther staring and gave her a small smile. Looking in this direction, Esther realized her own children were in the pew beside her. As she gazed at them, a baby behind her began to wail. The sound of it made her heart leap. When was the last time she'd heard a baby in church? She turned to look at the infant, who had been handed off to a grandmother now, who gently rocked her arms from side to side. The baby stopped crying and started trying to grab the feathers that sprang out of her grandmother's hatband. Hiding her laughter, Esther turned front again as a candy wrapper rustled nearby and a mother shushed her child. Somewhere, someone snored softly. Esther had forgotten how beautiful a full sanctuary could sound.

The service ended, and Russell stood, still holding her hand. He let several people pass and then stepped into the aisle. He paused and motioned for her to go first. She did, but she slid her left hand into his before letting go with her right. She didn't want to let go of his hand. She didn't want to let go of him. She didn't trust him not to disappear again.

After checking to make sure her children were following, she led them outside into the brilliant sunshine and the smell of freshly cut grass and instantly she recognized the street. It was the street she lived on now, but it looked different. Some of the houses were different colors, and one of them was new altogether—or was it old?

The cars were old, but they looked shiny and new. She gasped and looked up at Russ. They were in a different time! How was this possible? Was she dreaming? If so, she didn't want to wake up. He looked so handsome.

Her phone rang, and she tried to ignore it. She knew then that this was a dream, and she didn't want to leave it. Looking at Russ's face, she saw the church behind him. It was the old one, the one that had been abandoned. But it didn't look old or abandoned now. It was grand with fresh paint and beautiful stained-glass windows still in their place. She gazed at it as her phone rang again.

"Go ahead," Russ said. He bent and kissed her lightly on the lips. "Answer the phone. It's important." And then he was gone.

It was all gone.

She groped for the phone as she opened her eyes. "Hello?" she said groggily. Her pillow was wet with her tears. She wiped at her eyes. "Hello?" she said again.

"Did I wake you?" Vicky asked.

Esther considered lying, but why bother? There was no shame in napping on a Sunday afternoon.

"It's all right. I usually nap on Sundays too, but I'm too upset to nap today. I'm mad as a hornet. I've been on the phone all afternoon, and I can't make heads or tails of this. I don't know what we're going to do!"

"I think we're all going to have to find another church." She knew she sounded sulky, but she didn't care.

"So that's it? You're just going to give up?"

"We could start our own church." The idea hadn't occurred to her until she spoke it aloud, but now her whole body broke out in goosebumps, and an unexpected hope settled over her.

Vicky guffawed. "Our own church? A bunch of old broads? I don't think so."

Esther sank back into her couch. "I'm not sure it would be that hard—"

"Hard? They're not going to let us use that building! They just told me they're going to sell it!"

"We don't need that building—"

"What? Are we going to meet in your apartment? Maybe three of us could fit in there! And you can't meet here—you'll freeze to death!"

Esther rolled her eyes. No one would freeze to death in the summer, but Vicky rattled around in an old farmhouse that was practically falling down around her. It took a lot of wood to keep it warm in the winters, and Vicky was a cheapskate.

"No, we'll meet in a church. Let me make some calls."

"Make some calls? Who are you going to call?"

"I'll talk to you soon. Bye—"

"Wait!"

Esther paused.

Vicky let out a long breath. "Look, I don't want to join another church, and isn't starting our own church essentially the same thing?"

"Not at all," Esther said quickly.

"Why not?"

"We will *never* agree on which church to join." She'd known these women for decades. They couldn't even agree on a curtain color. "We find a new church, we scatter. We start a new church, we stay together."

Chapter 7

Emma

Sick to her stomach, Emma rested the still-hot wild berry pie on Mrs. Patterson's porch railing so she could knock on the door. She'd never been this close to the house, and she felt as if she were violating her privacy. She picked the pie up again, wishing it didn't smell so good. She hoped Mrs. Patterson wouldn't answer. She was relieved that both Raven and Natalie had declined her invitation to participate in this forced apology.

They waited for an eternity.

Her mother reached over her shoulder and knocked on the door, which annoyed Emma immensely. What, her knock hadn't been good enough? Her mother had a superior knock?

"Mrs. Patterson?" her mother called out in her fake, singsong church voice. "We don't want to bother you, but my daughter would like to apologize."

They heard a scraping sound from inside, and Emma's stomach flipped. Was the woman actually going to answer the door?

No. Apparently, she wasn't.

Emma shifted her weight to her other foot. In her peripheral vision, she saw a curtain flick. She looked in that direction, but saw only curtain. "I don't think she's coming."

"I don't think so either. Mrs. Patterson! We've made you a pie! We'll leave it right here on your porch. And we're very sorry for what the girls did. They didn't mean any harm."

This was not true. Why was her mother lying?

Emma turned to go, even though her mother hadn't budged yet. "Come on," she said under her breath.

"Put the pie down first."

Emma looked down at the peeling paint. "Here?"

"Yes, she'll come get it."

Emma wasn't so sure, and this seemed a great waste of pie. But getting out of there was more important than the pie, so she put the dessert down and then tried to herd her mother down the steps. Then she had a strong urge and without thinking about it so that she could talk herself out of it, she turned back to the door. "I'm really sorry, Mrs. Patterson! I know it was stupid, and I tried to talk them out of it. I'm sorry that I failed." When the words had flown out of her, the tightness in her chest went with them. "You didn't deserve to be harassed like that," she added, more softly. "I hope you enjoy the pie."

She turned and went down the steps, for the first time understanding her mother's obsession with always involving baked goods. She'd always thought it was silly, and maybe it was, but it was *something*. Something real, something people could touch, something that said they mattered.

As they walked, her mother slid her arm around her shoulders and pulled her closer. "I'm so, so proud of you, honey. I love you."

"I love you too. And I now get why you love to bake."

Her mother laughed shrilly. "Oh, honey. I *hate* to bake."

This was a startling revelation, and Emma waited for her to say more, but she didn't.

"I think I want to work harder at avoiding Isabelle. I know she goes to our church and everything, but I really hate her."

Her mother stopped walking and turned to face her.

Emma's heart sank. They'd almost been home. So close.

"Emma, honey, you can't hate Isabelle."

Of course she couldn't. Why had she said that out loud?

"Hating Isabelle doesn't hurt her."

Emma had to concentrate on not rolling her eyes. Of course it didn't hurt Isabelle. When had she said that it did? She didn't care about hurting Isabelle. She didn't care anything *about* Isabelle. She hated her too much to care.

"Hating Isabelle only hurts you." Her mother grabbed her gently by her upper arms and gazed down into her eyes.

"I know that," she muttered.

"I know you do."

Her mother kissed her on the forehead and released her, making Emma wonder if the whole hatred speech had been a reflex. She had said the word hate, meaning her Christian mother *had* to give her the hatred-is-bad speech, and now they could move on. Her mother was already over it and walking again. Emma caught up.

"But I do love the idea of avoiding her. In fact, I didn't tell you, but this morning, Mary Sue's mother invited you on a camping trip."

There was a reason her mother didn't look at her when she said this. She knew how she would react. Mary Sue was the biggest weirdo in church. Avoiding Isabelle didn't mean she had to go camping with the likes of Mary Sue.

"I don't think that's such a good idea." Her mind raced for an excuse. "I don't even like camping."

They reached the edge of their driveway, and her mother stopped walking. "I shouldn't have said camping *trip*," she hurriedly added. "They're camping in their backyard. Mary Sue is having a few friends over, and they're going to have a campfire and roast marshmallows."

Emma suppressed a groan. This kept getting worse. "A few friends? Who?" Mary Sue didn't have any friends except her siblings.

"I don't know. Friends from church, I would imagine."

Emma snickered. "Mom, Mary Sue doesn't have any friends from church."

Her mother didn't argue.

"And she doesn't have any friends from school because she doesn't *go* to school. And she doesn't do sports. She doesn't do *anything*."

"I don't know, honey. I didn't give her an answer, but I think you should do it. How bad can it be? You might find out you like her. She's a nice girl, and they're a nice family. And it sounds like there's lots to do on their farm."

"Their farm?" She hadn't even known they lived on a farm, and now she was starting to panic. "Like what? Milk the cows?"

"I don't think they have cows. I think they milk their goats."

"Goats?" Emma cried. "Gross! I don't want to milk goats! I don't want to do anything with goats!"

Her mother laughed, and this annoyed her. This wasn't funny. "Let's go inside. The mosquitoes are eating me alive. But I want you to do it. I'm going to tell Mrs. Puddy that you accept the invitation."

Chapter 8

Tonya

"What was all that with Emma today?"

The question surprised Tonya. Roy rarely noticed anything that was happening with their daughter, or, if he did, he rarely commented on it.

She wasn't sure whether she should answer him. She thought the question might be a trap. She didn't know how yet, but this could probably become her fault.

"Isabelle Martin played a prank on Mrs. Patterson today. Emma felt bad about it, so she and I made Mrs. Patterson a pie and apologized."

He hesitated and then, somewhat absentmindedly, said, "That doesn't sound like Isabelle."

Tonya bit her tongue.

Roy didn't say anything for the longest time, and she thought the conversation was over. But after he stood and announced he was going to bed, he asked, "Did Mrs. Patterson open the door?"

"No," Tonya said sadly. "She did not."

Roy walked away without another word, without saying good night, and she watched television for a while before heading for the laundry room. She kept a lot of her clothes in there. It was easier than carrying them around the house. She changed into her pajamas and then headed for the guest room. Emma, who was standing in front of the fridge, watched her coming down the hallway. She looked sad.

Tonya paused with her hand on the doorknob. "You okay, honey?"

"Yeah," she said, but it was clear she wasn't.

"You know that you can tell me anything?"

"Yeah, I know." She turned back to the fridge.

"Good night, honey. Don't eat anything too sugary."

"I won't," she said without pulling her head out of the fridge.

A bit mystified but too tired to worry too much about it, Tonya went into the small bedroom and closed the door behind her. She flicked on the lamp on the nightstand and then pulled back the covers and climbed between the sheets, which felt cool and comforting.

She settled in and turned the light off. Moonlight shone through the window, lighting the whole room. How long had she been sleeping in this room? She tried to remember when it had started and let out a little gasp when she realized it had been nearly a year. She couldn't believe it. The first few nights, she'd thought it would only be for a few nights. She almost laughed at the naivety of her year-ago self.

When she'd realized she wouldn't be welcomed back into her bedroom anytime soon, she'd been heartbroken, and then bitter. But, as the months went on, she'd grown comfortable with the idea, and then grateful.

It had started when she'd had a bad cold and was having trouble breathing. Roy had claimed he couldn't sleep with her snoring and that he didn't want to get overtired and then catch what she had. He hadn't asked her to sleep in the guest room, but he'd made it clear he didn't want her sleeping beside him. Then he'd spent the following days celebrating how much better he slept without her "pushing him out of bed." This unfair accusation had made her angry. It was true that, in the beginning of their marriage, she did tend to travel across the bed because her sleeping self liked to cuddle up to someone she loved. But he'd made it clear early on that he didn't like to be touched while he was sleeping, and somehow, she had trained herself to perch on the edge of the bed. So now, all these years later, to be told she'd never made the effort made her steaming mad. This anger made it easier to stay in the guest bedroom, and the longer she stayed in the guest bedroom, the easier it got. After a few weeks, she noticed that she too slept better alone—probably because she wasn't subconsciously trying to stay perched on the bed's border all night.

She shook her head. What was she doing? Why was she thinking about her marriage again? There was no use. She rolled onto her side and pulled the blankets up to her chin, grateful that the failure of her marriage didn't hurt anymore. In the beginning, it had hurt. A lot.

Chapter 9

Esther

On Monday morning, Esther wiped off her tablet and opened a browser. Her daughter had bought the tablet for her so she could have some online face time with her grandchildren. But her grandchildren never used the app, so the tablet mostly served as a dust collector.

A quick search revealed the old church and showed some interior photographs that made Esther gasp. The pictures were dark and shadowy, and the sanctuary was full of junk, but it was still easy to see how grand the church had once been. The ceiling looked to be nigh fifty feet high, and yet it barely cleared the top of the pipe organ.

The asking price was far lower than Esther had expected, and she wondered if she could sell the pipe organ to pay for the building. It would be a shame to part the two, but none of the seven of them could play the thing, and she didn't think they'd be hiring an organist anytime soon.

Her heart drumming, she called Vicky.

It was Vicky's turn to be woken by the phone.

"Sorry to wake you," Esther said, even though she wasn't really sorry. It wasn't even that early. Vicky should have been up an hour ago. "I have an idea."

"All right."

Esther could hear her dragging herself to a seated position.

"What is it?"

"You want to take a few minutes and then call me back?" Esther figured she needed to use the bathroom and get some coffee.

"You trying to kill me with the suspense?"

Esther chuckled. "All right. You know that old church down the street from my building?"

She hesitated. "You mean the Baptist one?"

"No, that's on the next street over. The one on my street. The vacant one."

"I don't think there's a church on your street."

Esther sighed, trying to be patient. "I think I know whether there's a church on my street. I can see it from my window." This wasn't entirely true.

"Your window faces Main Street."

"I meant the window from the hallway."

"Fine. What about it?"

This wasn't good enough. "It's a few doors down. It sits off the street a little, has a big lawn that is all grown up now. I don't think it's been used since the seventies."

"Oh, good grief, the roof is probably caved in."

"I don't think so. Things were built to last back then, remember? And I'm looking at pictures of it right now, and it doesn't look to be in too bad a shape. It needs to be cleaned out and spruced up, of course—"

"Pictures? Where did you get pictures?"

"I'm on the real estate website."

Vicky was quiet for a minute, and Esther gave her a chance to let it sink in. "So what's your plan?"

"It's not that much money. If we pooled our resources, I think we could do it."

"Resources? What resources? None of us have any money."

Esther didn't know whether this was true. She had a little. Not enough, but a little. "Maybe we should meet and talk about it."

"Fine. McDonald's. Ten o'clock. Call the others." Vicky hung up.

Esther would have been offended, but she figured the grace period on Vicky's trip to the bathroom was close to expiring. She put the phone down and looked at the picture. They could do this, couldn't they? *Shouldn't* they? She called the others and invited them to coffee without telling them why.

"I don't have any money," Cathy said.

This was bad news. If she couldn't afford a cup of McDonald's coffee, she probably wasn't going to pitch in to buy a church.

"I'll buy your breakfast."

"You don't need to do that. I had my breakfast hours ago."

"Cathy, please come. I'll buy you something if you want it, but either way, we need you there."

Cathy hesitated. "This sounds serious. What's going on, Esther?"

"I'll tell you when you get there."

"Tell me now or I'm not coming."

Esther put her head in her hands. "Fine." She filled her in and then waited for the onslaught of arguments, but they didn't come.

Cathy was quiet for a minute and then said, "See you at ten, and I'll take you up on that offer. I'll call it my lunch."

Chapter 10

Esther

All seven ladies were on time. Esther hadn't been keeping track over the last few decades, but still, she thought this was a first. They stood in line for what felt like an unreasonable amount of time, and then, one by one, they turned with their trays and went to their usual spot. Vera had trouble carrying a tray because of her cane, so Esther grabbed hers and then left her behind, eager to get to the table. But then she felt guilty and waited for Vera to catch up.

Vera had reached the table, but hadn't sat down yet, when Vicky announced, "Esther thinks we should buy the old church on her street and start a new church."

Everyone but Cathy gasped.

"Tell them how much it is," Vicky ordered without looking at Esther.

Esther took a deep breath. "Twenty-five thousand."

"Twenty-five thousand dollars?" Vera cried. "For what?"

Esther got her caught up as the others fired questions at Vicky. When there was finally a lull, Vicky said, "I appreciate your enthusiasm, Esther. I do. But this is not practical. And even if it were, I don't think it's possible."

Esther scanned their faces. "Nothing is impossible with God."

Vicky blew out a puff of air. "That verse was written for young people! Look around you! We don't have the money. But even if we did, then what? How are we going to repair the building? We can't do it ourselves, and we can't afford to hire help. Then we'll have to heat the building. That will cost a fortune. And for what? There are only seven of us! Do we really need that giant money pit so that the seven of us can continue to eat muffins together on Sunday?"

Esther was genuinely angry with Vicky, but she tried not to let it show. "It won't be the seven of us," she said slowly. "We'll be starting a church. Others will come, and—"

"Who?" Vicky cried. "Who will come? No one came to our old church. That's how we got shut down! Why would anyone come to this one? We don't even have a pastor!" She pretended to slap herself on the forehead. "I hadn't even thought of that! How are we going to pay a pastor? And where are we going to find one? It takes real churches months, sometimes even years, to find a pastor to move to remote rural Maine. How are we going to do it?"

It appeared that everyone was agreeing with Vicky, and Esther started to feel discouraged. Maybe this wasn't going to work after all. "I don't know," Esther said. "I don't know the answer to any of these questions, but we can't just do nothing."

At first no one said anything, but then Cathy quietly said, "We could do things differently."

"What?" Vicky snapped. "Speak up!"

Cathy straightened up in her seat, but her voice remained soft. "We got shut down at our church. But we could do things differently at a new one."

"It's not *our* fault we got shut down," Vicky said.

"Give her a chance to talk!" Dawn said and then looked at Cathy expectantly.

"I'm not saying that we did anything wrong. But we did get shut down for a reason. And you're right, Vicky. We got together every Sunday and we ate muffins. That's it. What else did we do? When was the last time we did anything with or for the community? When was the last time any of us even invited anyone to church—"

"I don't invite people because they never come," Vicky said. "People don't like church anymore. No one in these generations goes to church."

"That's not true, and you know it," Cathy said, her voice growing stronger. "We've all driven by churches with full parking lots. But I'm not even saying we want a full parking lot."

This was good, as the building on her street didn't even *have* a parking lot.

"We don't need a megachurch," Cathy continued. "But it wouldn't be the seven of us unless we wanted it to be. People are still hungry for God. If we reach out to them, they will come."

Esther wanted to hug Cathy. She had so clearly articulated ideas that Esther hadn't even realized were on her own heart. "Amen!" she said too loudly for McDonald's and then looked around self-consciously.

"Fine. It's a great idea," Vicky said sarcastically. "But we still can't afford it."

"We don't know that yet," Esther said. "I think that those of us who want to do it should have an honest conversation about how much we can each afford to contribute." She was interested to hear Dawn's answer to that question. She knew Dawn wasn't rich, but she was better off than the rest of them, and she appeared intrigued by the idea. "So, first, who is interested?"

Vicky folded her arms across her chest.

"I'm in," Cathy said quickly. She wished Cathy had a bigger bank account, one that matched her enthusiasm, but she supposed that if she had to choose between money and enthusiasm, she would choose the latter.

"I'm in too," Dawn said.

"I'm in," Vera said.

Barbara looked around nervously. "I might be in?"

For the first time, Rachel spoke. "I might be in too."

Vicky dropped her arms. "Fine. For the sake of conversation, I'll say that I'm in, but there's really nothing to be *in*. We still aren't going to have enough money."

"I have a thousand dollars to contribute," Esther said boldly. She actually had a mite less than that, but she wanted to make a grand offer to inspire others, and she figured God would somehow provide the other seventy-five-ish dollars to get her up to the even thousand.

"A thousand dollars?" Vicky said. "How can you have a thousand dollars?"

"It's in my savings account. It's all I have."

Vicky looked horrified.

"I'm sorry," Barbara said. "I don't have any money, but I do have a handyman son. I'm sure he would help with fixing the place up."

"Thank you for volunteering Kyle," Esther said. "That will be wonderful. But you should contribute something financially as well. I'm not pressuring you, but I know that if you're truly in, you have *some* money to give."

"You *are* pressuring her then," Vicky said and patted Barbara's arm reassuringly.

Barbara subtly slid her arm out from under Vicky's touch. "I could come up with a hundred dollars."

Vicky glared at Esther. "Are you saying everyone has to contribute? That they can't be part of this if they don't give you money?"

"Of course not. And they're not giving *me* money. I think we should all contribute because we're all invested, but it's more than that. I feel like ..." Her brain searched for the right words. "I feel it's a spiritual thing. I feel like we all need to be spiritually invested, and where our money goes, that's where our heart is. It's an outward act of an inward commitment." She wished she could explain herself more clearly.

Vicky rolled her eyes.

Cathy took a sip of her gifted coffee. "Well said, Esther. I understand completely. If we're going to do this, we have to commit entirely."

"Do this?" Vicky cried. "Who said we're committing to anything? I thought we were just talking!"

Cathy ignored her completely and looked at Dawn. "How much can you contribute?"

"I can do a thousand too."

Esther almost slapped the table with excitement.

Cathy looked at Vera. "And you?"

"I could probably give fifty dollars."

Cathy nodded and then looked at Rachel. "And you?"

Rachel looked like a scared rabbit. "Would twenty dollars help?"

"Of course," Cathy said quickly.

Rachel nodded. "Twenty dollars then."

Cathy looked at Vicky. "And you?"

"Does it really matter? We're still about twenty-two thousand dollars short."

"Does that mean you don't want to chip in?" Cathy asked.

"That's not what I said." She pursed her lips. "I can do a hundred dollars. But like I said, *still twenty-two thousand dollars short.*"

Cathy let out a long breath and smiled at Vicky. "I'd like to contribute twenty-two thousand dollars."

Chapter 11

Emma

E mma did *not* want to go "camping" at Mary Sue Puddy's house, and she was furious that her mother was making her. She'd done just fine ignoring Isabelle all week. She didn't need a forced friendship with Mary Sue to help her avoid Isabelle, and she told her mother as much.

Her mother wouldn't listen.

Instead, her mother drove her deep into the woods and then down a long, bumpy gravel driveway.

"Mom, I might die out here."

Her mother laughed. "I doubt it."

"No really. A black bear is going to get me. Or maybe a sasquatch."

She laughed again, sounding annoyingly joyful. "I think the mosquitoes might be a bigger threat."

"That's not funny."

"Did you bring your bug dope?"

"No."

"Then you're right. It's not funny." She stopped in front of a giant ugly farmhouse.

Emma decided to try one more time. "Mom, *please* don't make me do this! Please, please, please!"

Her mother leaned over and kissed her on the cheek. "I won't make you do it again. I think you might have fun. If you don't, then I'll apologize later."

Emma mustered her strongest glare, hoping her wrath would persuade her mother to reason.

It didn't.

Mary Sue came running out of the house trailed by her siblings, multiple dogs, and a chicken.

Emma groaned, put on a fake smile, and climbed out of the car. "Hey, Mary Sue."

"Thanks for coming!" Mary Sue grabbed her hand and started pulling her. "Come on, I want you to meet the goats!"

Emma heard her mother get out of the car and greet Mary Sue's mother, and her heart ached to be back with her mother, but she was being pulled toward a goat barn.

Mary Sue ripped the old wooden door open so hard that Emma was surprised it didn't fall off. Mary Sue pulled her inside and pointed.

Oh, wow. They *were* pretty cute. "They're so small!"

"Yep! They're Nigerian Dwarf Goats! They're from West Africa! Well, *these* goats aren't from West Africa. They're from Damariscotta, but the *breed* is from West Africa. Originally. They're wicked soft! Go ahead and pet them!" She reached over the wooden rail and ran her hand down one of the goat's backs. "This is Rubis!"

Tentatively, Emma reached over the rail and touched the goat, who nuzzled her head into her hand like a dog. Emma gasped. "She *is* soft!" Then she felt stupid. "She *is* a girl, right?"

"Of course she's a girl!"

"Oh. Well, Rubis sounds kind of like a boy name."

"Nope. Rubis is ruby in French."

"Oh. Do you speak French?"

"We're learning! *Est-ce que tu parles français?*"

"Uh ... what?"

Mary Sue giggled and pointed. "That one there is Batwoman, and that one is Sweet Pepper, and that one is Ruth, and that there is Bigfoot."

Ah, so there *was* a Bigfoot on the premises. Emma looked at her. "You sure do get excited about your goats."

Mary Sue tittered. "I love them! They're my pets! And they feed me!"

Emma reeled back. "You *eat* them?"

Mary Sue laughed and elbowed her in the ribs. "No, silly. They are *dairy* goats. They feed me milk and cheese. You want some?"

Emma looked at the goats nervously. "Want some what?"

"Fresh milk!"

Despite her reservations, Emma was enjoying Mary Sue's unbridled joy. She didn't know anyone who enjoyed life this much. "Um, no thank you."

Mary Sue looked disappointed. "You sure?"

She wasn't sure about anything. "I'm sure."

One of Mary Sue's brothers had climbed over the railing.

"Victor! Get out of there!"

Victor ignored her.

Mary Sue rolled her eyes.

Emma heard the crunching gravel that meant her mother was pulling away, but only a slight panic fluttered through her. She felt much better about the evening ahead. "Do you have the tent set up yet?"

Mary Sue's face lit up. "Yes! Want to see it?"

Emma laughed. "Sure!"

Mary Sue grabbed her hand and pulled her out of the barn. Victor scrambled back over the rail to follow them.

"Are all your brothers and sisters camping with us too?"

Mary Sue leaned into her. "Oh, no way! Don't worry!"

"No, that's not what I meant. It would be okay if they did. I like little kids. I was just wondering."

"I like little kids too," Mary Sue said quickly. "But no, they're not camping with us. There wouldn't be room."

A tent came into view, and it was huge. Emma thought that there would be plenty of room, but she didn't say anything.

"Shoes off!" Mary Sue ordered when they reached the tent. She bent to unzip the flap, and Emma slipped her flip-flops off.

Mary Sue dove into the tent, and Emma followed with a little less confidence.

"Wow! This is cool!" It reminded her of the forts she and her mother used to build in their living room.

Mary Sue scrunched up her face. "Haven't you ever been camping before?"

Emma shook her head. "No, I haven't. Don't even really know how to camp." Normally, she would feel stupid admitting something like this, but she was feeling very safe with Mary Sue.

Mary Sue grinned. "No worries! I'll teach you everything you need to know."

They heard crunching gravel again, and Mary Sue climbed back out of the tent.

With some reluctance, Emma followed her, and what she saw next brought tears to her eyes. A giant, shiny SUV had just pulled into the Puddys' driveway.

"Is that ...?"

"Yes," Mary Sue said sadly. She looked at Emma. "I'm sorry. My mother made me."

Isabelle had arrived, and Emma didn't feel so safe anymore.

Chapter 12

Esther

The ladies had offered the asking price, and their offer had been accepted. Now they were stepping into their new sanctuary for the first time.

Esther gasped. The pictures hadn't done it justice.

"It smells like mold," Vicky said.

"No, it doesn't," Esther snapped.

"It smells like a new beginning," Cathy said.

"You know," Esther said, "that would be a great name for the church."

"What?" Cathy said. "New Beginning? A little on the nose, don't you think?"

Esther laughed. "How about New Beginnings?" She emphasized the plural. "Everyone who steps inside can have a brand-new beginning every time they step inside."

"I love it," Vera said. "We're going to have to build a wheelchair ramp, pronto."

"Why?" Vicky said. "You don't use a wheelchair."

"Won't be long," Vera said quietly.

"Wow, look at the organ!" Rachel said in wonder.

"I was thinking we could sell that," Esther said. "It's got to be worth a fortune. It might pay for all the repairs we need."

"If it was worth a fortune, don't you think they would have sold it already?" Vicky said.

"I don't think we should sell it," Rachel said. "I think we should play it."

"Maybe, but I think we would need to pay an organist," Esther said.

Rachel stepped up onto the organ's platform. "I don't think we should sell it."

Fearing this would be the first point of contention, Esther dropped it.

Rachel ran her fingers down the keys and sighed. "But you're right. We could probably use the money more than we can use the organ. I'll look into selling it."

"Thank you," Esther said.

"We're lucky they left the pews," Barbara said.

Esther didn't think luck had anything to do with it.

"When are we closing again?" Barbara said, looking to Esther for the answer.

"Tuesday, but the owners said we can move in anytime."

Vicky snickered. "Move in," she repeated derisively.

"I mean we can start getting the place ready."

Vicky shook her head. "I still don't see how we can do all this. Just *look* at how much work there is."

Esther looked around and tried to be objective. There *were* some issues. The windows were all boarded up, the wallpaper was peeling, and there was a foot of dust on everything. She had no idea what shape the wiring or plumbing was in.

"Kyle is ready to start anytime," Barbara said.

"Stop trying to drum up business for your son!" Vicky said. "The minute he demanded we pay him was the minute he became not much use to us."

"Stop," Esther said sharply.

Vicky looked at her, her eyes wide.

"Either get with us or leave, Vicky!" Her own boldness surprised her. "You are doing us more harm than you know! I love you. We all love you. But if you don't want to be a part of this, then don't be a part of it. You can still come to church here, even. But if you don't want to be a part of getting us going, then please leave us alone!"

Vicky didn't respond. Her obvious indignation had apparently rendered her speechless.

"She's right," Cathy said softly. "We do love you, Vicky. But we don't need your negativity. We are going to do this, and if we fail, we fail. That will be okay. But we're going to try." She looked at Barbara. "Tell Kyle we're ready for him." She turned to Esther. "We need to make a list of what we want him to do."

"I would say he needs to check the electrical and plumbing first. I have no idea how to do any of that."

Vicky let out a long sigh. "Have you all forgotten my son Alex is a plumber? I'll give him a call. And I won't let him charge us."

"Great," Cathy said. "Thank you, Vicky."

"The closing is Tuesday?" Rachel said.

"That's the plan," Esther said.

Vicky sighed. "When is our first service?"

The question sent a thrill through Esther. "How about the twenty-eighth?"

"Of July?" Vicky screeched. "We'll never be ready!" Her expression softened. "Sorry, didn't mean to sound critical."

Esther bit back a laugh. "The building will not be perfect, but we don't need it to be. We need to put a sign outside and make sure the toilet works. I think we can do those two things before the twenty-eighth."

"Uh ... who is going to preach?" Vicky asked.

At first no one said anything.

"I'll pray about it," Esther said, "and I'll try to find someone to be a guest preacher."

"Or I could do it," Cathy said.

They all looked at her, surprised.

"You're a woman!" Vicky said.

Cathy frowned. "We're *all* women."

"But a man might come!"

Esther held up her hand to stave off the next argument. "Fine. Cathy can preach." She couldn't imagine it, but crazier things had happened.

"We need to come up with our doctrinal statement," Rachel said.

Esther didn't like the sound of that.

"So we know where we stand on things. Will this church allow female preachers? Will we sprinkle or dunk? Wine or grape juice?"

Barbara groaned. "There is so much to do."

Esther rubbed her hands together. "I know. Isn't it great? Let's get started!"

Chapter 13

Emma

"Let's go for a bike ride!" Mary Sue suggested.

"I don't have my bike," Isabelle said.

"We have loads of bikes. You can borrow one of ours."

Isabelle looked at the old, banged-up bikes scattered around the Puddys' lawn and scrunched up her nose. "I don't *want* to ride one of your bikes."

"Do you want to play Hide and Seek?" Mary Sue tried.

"Hide and Seek is for babies."

Mary Sue gave Emma a tired look. She had suggested over a dozen activities, and Isabelle had pooh-poohed every one of them. Why had she come? Emma had been right on the edge of having actual fun for the first time that summer, and then Isabelle had reappeared like her personal poltergeist.

"What do *you* want to do?" Mary Sue asked.

"Do you have the Hollywood Life app on your phone?"

Emma wanted to slap her. Isabelle knew that Mary Sue didn't have a smart phone.

But Mary Sue didn't appear to be hurt by Isabelle's barb. "Nope, sure don't."

Isabelle rolled her eyes and looked at Emma. "Did you bring *your* phone?"

"We're not going to play with our phones, Isabelle."

"Fine. Let's play Truth or Dare."

Mary Sue looked uncomfortable, but she agreed.

"Great! Let's go into the woods!" And before they could argue, she ran toward the trees.

Mary Sue took off after her, and Emma grudgingly followed.

Night was falling, and the mosquitoes were thicker when they got into the trees. Isabelle dramatically slapped at her legs. "Ew! Bugs are so *gross!*" She looked at Mary Sue. "Truth or dare?"

Mary Sue slapped at the back of her neck. "I'm going back to the yard. Come on, Emma."

Beyond grateful, Emma followed Mary Sue back to the yard.

"Supper!" Mary Sue's mom called from the doorway and then popped back inside.

"Oh, good. I'm hungry."

Emma followed Mary Sue inside to find most of her family already seated around the giant table.

"Wash up, girls." Her mom looked toward the open doorway. "Where's Isabelle?"

"In the woods," Mary Sue said nonchalantly.

"The woods?" Her mom headed toward the door. "You left her in the woods?"

Mary Sue scowled. "It's not like she'll get lost. She was like ten feet from the lawn."

Her mom scanned the property and then said, "Victor, go find her."

Victor popped up and ran for the door.

Hoping Isabelle was lost for good, Emma washed her hands and then followed Mary Sue to the table. She was starving, and the food smelled amazing.

Everyone was seated, but no one was touching the food, and Emma realized they were waiting for Victor and Isabelle. Now she hoped her nemesis would be found, so that she could eat.

Sure enough, Isabelle came through the door glaring at Mary Sue. "I got lost out there!" she accused. "And it's dark out!"

It wasn't dark out, not yet, and there was no way she'd gotten lost, unless it had been on purpose.

"She was still ten feet from the lawn," Victor said, and some of the little ones giggled.

Isabelle's face turned red with fury, and her hands tightened into fists.

Emma glanced at Mary Sue, a bit worried about the revenge that Isabelle would soon rain on Emma's new friend. But Mary Sue was oblivious to the threat, and Emma had a new thought: What *could* Isabelle do to Mary Sue? She couldn't embarrass her because Mary Sue didn't care what Isabelle's people thought. And she couldn't affect Mary Sue's social life because Mary Sue didn't have one. Emma almost snickered at the thought. One thing was clear: she needed to be more like Mary Sue.

Mary Sue's father said grace, and then they dug in. The food was amazing, and Emma finally got to try goat milk. It was delicious. Isabelle hardly ate anything, claiming to be a vegan, even though this was a total lie. No one seemed offended by her impromptu veganism; the Puddys enjoyed their meal around her little single-actor play.

Emma ate till she was full and then ate some more. Then she followed Mary Sue and her father back to the tent with Isabelle trailing behind. Emma didn't know why Mr. Puddy was along until he started to build a fire. Emma actually got excited about this and sat down on a rock to watch the process.

Soon, the kindling was crackling, and the flames were leaping. "Have fun, girls. Let us know if you need anything."

When he was out of sight, Isabelle said, "Finally! Now, Mary Sue, *truth or dare.*"

Mary Sue rolled her eyes, but the prospect of playing this game seemed more exciting in the dark.

"Truth, I guess."

Without hesitation, Isabelle asked, "Who do you have a crush on?"

"Do *not* answer that!"

Isabelle's head snapped toward her. "Why would you say that? You can't say that!"

"She will tell *everyone.*"

Mary Sue winked at Emma. "I don't mind. It's not a secret. I have a crush on Richard Bastille."

Emma giggled. Richard Bastille was an eighty-something-year-old who sat in the back row of their church.

"Who?" Isabelle cried.

Mary Sue started giggling too, and Isabelle grew angry.

"Emma!" Isabelle snapped. "Truth or dare?"

For some reason, this made Emma laugh even harder. Was this possible? Were she and Mary Sue *ganging up on* Isabelle? Had anyone ganged up on Isabelle before? Was that even possible? How was it that here in the middle of nowhere on a weird farm with a weird family that Isabelle had no power?

"Fine! You choose *truth.* Emma, tell the truth! Do you know that your pastor father is having sex with Jason DeGrave's mother?"

Chapter 14

Emma

Mary Sue abruptly stopped laughing. "Isabelle," she said without breathing, "don't."

Emma's stomach fell out of her, and she felt dizzy. "What did you say?"

Isabelle smirked, and suddenly the campfire wasn't pretty. Suddenly the firelight made Isabelle's face look like a demon.

"I *said*, do you know that your father the pastor is boinking Alexis DeGrave?"

Somehow, Emma felt hot and cold at the same time. "No, he's not." She couldn't breathe.

"*That* isn't the question. The fact is that he *is*. The question is *do you know?*"

This wasn't true. This was absurd. But then Emma looked at Mary Sue, and the tears streaming down her face told her she was wrong. This *was* true. Mary Sue couldn't even look at her.

Emma got to her feet, her legs shaking.

"You haven't answered the question. If you don't answer the question, you get a *double* truth, and the double truth is, does your mother know?"

Emma walked away into the darkness with no idea where she was going. When the tears started coming, she turned to see that Isabelle wasn't following her. But neither was Mary Sue.

It was true. It couldn't be. But it was. And now that the idea was planted in her head, hadn't part of her known it all along? Hadn't she seen the way her father looked at Mrs. DeGrave? Hadn't she seen the way she looked at him? All the clues were there. Her father's many late-night ministry calls. The fact that Mr. DeGrave didn't come to church. The fact that her mother slept in the guest room. Did her mother *know*? That idea filled her with more horror than the affair itself. Surely her mother wouldn't *let* her husband cheat on her and not do anything about it! But no, her father wouldn't do this. This was all some horrible mistake. Her father was a pastor, for crying out loud. Then she remembered Mary Sue's face. And her tears.

This was true.

This was the most horrible truth she'd ever heard, and it had been delivered by the lips of Isabelle Martin. Of course it had.

She realized she had stopped walking. She was standing in the middle of the Puddys' lawn, and the mosquitoes were biting her. She reached toward her back pocket for her phone, but who was she going to call? She couldn't talk to either of her parents right now. What was she going to do? Where was she going to go? She would rather bleed to death in a mosquito field than go back to that campfire.

Her eyes landed on a bike lying in the grass a few feet in front of her. It was as good a plan as any. She went to it, stood it upright, and climbed on. Her mother would kill her for riding without a helmet, but the idea of making her mother angry felt mighty good right now.

Emma started pedaling and soon she was sailing down the bumpy driveway. The moon was bright, so she could see where she was going, and she pedaled even harder, going faster and faster, knowing she was in danger and not caring; the danger made her feel better, and she pedaled as hard as she could, until the sweat rolled down her back and the tears rolled down her face.

Not realizing she had reached the end of the driveway, she raced out into the dirt road and straight across it into the ditch. The front wheel of her bike crashed into the bank, and she sailed over the handlebars, too angry to be afraid. She landed in a crumpled ball, and then she wailed. She screamed in pain, not for her now-injured shoulder—she could hardly feel that pain—but for her heart, for her life. Everything she knew had just come crashing down around her. Her father wasn't a strong man of God. Her mother wasn't a strong woman. Her family was a sham, a joke, and the worst part of it was that *everyone knew*.

If Mary Sue Puddy knew, then *everyone knew*, because the Puddys didn't know anything. They weren't in any of the cliques, and no one gossiped to them. But Mary Sue had known.

Emma got to her hands and knees, threw up into the tall grass, and then rolled over again. She wanted to die. How could she face anyone ever again? How could she walk into her church? How could she face her friends? Did Raven and Natalie know too? Of course they did. No way would Isabelle not tell them. Emma realized she hardly cared about them. The real question was, how was she going to face her mother? Was she going to be the one to tell her? *Should* she tell her? Apparently, the whole town had decided she didn't need to know. Maybe Emma should just go that route. It might be easier. But no, she wouldn't do that. She couldn't do that. If her mother didn't know, then Emma couldn't let her continue to be the butt of all jokes. And if she did know, well then, Emma hated her and couldn't let her mother live without knowing it.

She realized that the mosquitoes were feasting on her again. She climbed out of the ditch, and her shoulder really started to hurt. She found the bike, climbed back on, and more slowly, started pedaling toward town. It hurt too much to hold on with her left hand, so she let it rest in her lap, and held on with only her right.

She wasn't even sure she could navigate back to town, but she didn't care. Maybe she'd end up in a different town, where no one knew her and her horrible lie of a family.

Chapter 15

Emma

Emma had no idea how long it had taken her to pedal back to town, but she was soaked with sweat. Though sobs continued to erupt without warning, her tears had dried up. Her shoulder throbbed. Her legs burned. She thought she might die of exhaustion, but she rode past the end of her street.

She wasn't going home.

She was going to the DeGraves' house.

She would have no idea where the stupid Alexis DeGrave lived and would definitely have no reason to care, but Alexis's son Jason was a gorgeous high school junior. She knew where Jason DeGrave lived. Everyone did. He was the soccer goalie, the center on the basketball team, and the first baseman, and every girl in high school was after him.

She pulled into their driveway and let the bike crash to the ground. For a second, her true self made an appearance. She paused. What was she doing? What would this accomplish? Fear flickered through her. But then anger pushed it out. She strode toward their fancy front door and then pounded on it. What time was it? She looked around town for clues, but all was still. There were no cars, no people walking. It was late.

She pounded on the door again.

It was ripped open, and suddenly she was staring up into the scary eyes of an angry man.

She jumped back. Why had *he* answered the door? She'd expected Alexis or Jason, but not this man. She'd never seen him before.

"What?" he barked.

"Who is it?" Jason asked from behind the man, and suddenly Jason DeGrave's voice was the sweetest thing she'd ever heard.

"Never mind. Get back to your room. Are you on drugs?"

She realized this last sentence had been directed at her and shook her head. "No, sir."

"Why are you pounding on my door in the middle of the night?"

Jason pushed into the doorway. "Dad! This is Emma Mendell." He laughed. "She's definitely not on drugs. Emma, what's wrong?"

The sincere concern in his voice made her stomach roll with guilt. She tried to speak but couldn't. She backed away and found her voice—sort of. "I'm sorry. I ... I ... made a mistake." She tripped, but found her footing, and continued backing away.

But then Alexis DeGrave appeared behind her husband, and Emma's rage returned. She stopped backing up.

"Emma?" Alexis said, and then her face fell. She had seen something in Emma. She knew that Emma knew. "Oh no," she said.

"What?" Mr. DeGrave said.

Emma looked at Jason, desperate to hurt someone, anyone. "Sorry to wake you up, Jason, but I just found out that your mother is sleeping with my father, and I came here to tell her that I hate her." She backed away again, and the further she got from the door, the louder her voice got, until she was shouting. "I came here to tell your mother that she's a slut!"

It felt *so* good to say that horrible word. She'd never said it, and she knew her parents would be horrified when they learned that she had. She picked up the Puddys' bike and started pedaling. She still didn't head toward home. She just kept pedaling, until an old pickup pulled up beside her. At first she thought she was about to be kidnapped, and terror gripped her. Suddenly, she wanted her mother more than she wanted anything in her life. But then she realized it was Mr. and Mrs. Puddy. She jumped off the bike, and it fell to the ground. Mrs. Puddy came running around the truck and wrapped her arms around her, and Emma let herself sink into those warm, motherly arms. "I'm sorry I took the bike," she mumbled into her shoulder.

Mrs. Puddy rubbed her back with a strong hand. "There, there. You can borrow our bikes anytime you want. You can borrow our anything anytime you want." She squeezed her even tighter. "Come on, child. Let's get you in the truck."

Emma nodded, and Mrs. Puddy let go of her. But she took her hand, just as Mary Sue had done earlier that evening. That felt like forever ago, and Emma wished she could go back.

The truck door stood open, and suddenly, Emma was too ashamed to climb in. She hung her head.

"Go ahead, honey."

Because Emma didn't know what else to do, she obeyed, and Mrs. Puddy climbed in behind her and put her arm around her shoulders. Emma wondered if the Puddys would adopt her. That would solve a lot of her problems. She wouldn't have to live with her parents. She wouldn't have to face Isabelle in school. They might even let her skip church.

Mr. Puddy pulled into Emma's driveway, and a fresh wave of tears erupted out of her. Part of her desperately wanted to be inside that familiar, comfortable home, but another part of her hated the sight of it.

"I'll go in first." Mr. Puddy unbuckled. He gave his wife a knowing look. "Make sure it's safe for her."

What? Why did they act like they knew what they were doing? Had they done this before? Was finding runaway bike thieves and returning them to their broken homes their thing?

Mr. Puddy didn't even make it to the door before her mother opened it. She came running out to the truck, and Mr. Puddy stepped into the house. Mrs. Puddy climbed out of the truck, and Emma allowed her mother to pull her out and wrap her arms around her.

"Oh, honey." Her mother was sobbing. "I was so scared."

Scared of what? Emma wondered.

Mrs. Puddy read her mind. "We called and told them you had left," she explained.

And yet the Puddys had been the ones to look for her, not her own parents?

She pulled away and looked up at her mother. "Did you know?"

"Did I know what?"

Emma looked at Mrs. Puddy, who read her mind again. "We didn't tell them the whole story."

Her mom frowned. "What whole story?"

Emma tried to keep her voice even. "Do you know about Mrs. DeGrave?"

Her mother's face fell, and she glanced over her shoulder at Mrs. Puddy. This infuriated Emma. *That* was her mother's reaction? Confronted by her daughter with the worst question possible, her first instinct was to worry about what Mrs. Puddy thought?

Unlike Mary Sue, Mrs. Puddy was able to meet the eyes of the accused. "You will get no judgment from me, Tonya," she said softly. "Whatever you need, I am here to help."

Her mother let go of her and stepped back. Emma tried to read her face, but there was nothing there.

Mr. Puddy appeared beside his wife. "They want us to go."

Mrs. Puddy looked at Tonya. "What about you? Do you want us to go?"

At first her mother didn't answer. Then she smiled sweetly and said, "We'll be just fine. Thank you, though."

Mrs. Puddy stepped toward her mother quickly and wrapped her arms around her. "Do you want to come home with us? We've got plenty of room."

Emma's heart leapt at the thought. Yes, Mom! Let's go live with the Puddys! That's the perfect solution.

"No, that's all right," she said in that same sticky-sweet voice. "Thank you for the offer, but we'll be just fine." She stepped away from the woman's embrace and possessively put her arm over Emma's shoulders. She squeezed Emma's left shoulder, and she cried out in pain and stepped away from her mother.

"Emma!" her mother cried. She sounded offended, but Emma thought she was mostly embarrassed.

"I believe Emma has a shoulder injury," Mrs. Puddy said softly.

"Come on, Lauren," Mr. Puddy said, and for the first time, Emma knew Mrs. Puddy's first name. And it was perfect. Lauren. What a beautiful name.

Lauren Puddy started to climb into the truck. "You call me, Tonya. Anytime, for anything." She shut the door behind her, and Mr. Puddy started the truck.

"Come on, let's go inside."

Emma didn't want to go inside, but she was too tired to do anything else, so she let herself be led to the door. They stepped into the living room to find her father standing by the window. "Have a seat, Emma. We need to talk."

Hate rolled through her so fast she thought she might burst into flames. "I don't want to talk to you."

"It can wait until morning, Roy. She's injured."

"What's wrong with her?"

"Are you blind? Her face is all skinned up, and her shoulder is hurt."

"How did you manage to hurt your shoulder?"

How do you manage to be mad at me for hurting my shoulder? "I was trying to kill myself." She wouldn't look at him, but still, she thought she saw him flinch, and this made her happy.

Her mother, though, cried out, and this did not make her happy. She looked at her mother, who suddenly looked so frail, so pathetic. "You still haven't answered my question." She asked it again with painful deliberateness. "Did ... you ... know?"

"No. Of course not." She looked at her husband, at her pastor. "Sort of, yes."

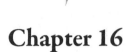

Chapter 16

Tonya

"You don't know anything!" Roy hollered. "None of this is true! I am under spiritual attack here, and I need you to defend me, not join with the darkness!"

Tonya thought she was going to be sick. Maybe she shouldn't have spent all those years pretending this couldn't happen. Pretending this wasn't happening. Maybe then it wouldn't be right in her face snarling at her. "Let's not do this in front of Emma."

"Do what in front of Emma? I can't defend myself in front of my daughter? You know what?" His voice grew louder, suddenly sounding more like his pulpit voice. "I think I need to defend myself *to* my daughter! Emma, explain yourself! Why are the Puddys calling me in the middle of the night and then showing up at my door with these accusations?"

Emma finally looked at her father, and the utter disappointment on her face broke Tonya's heart.

"Mom," Emma said softly, "I think we should leave."

Her father stepped closer. "No one is going anywhere!" his voice boomed. "Sit down!" He pointed at their couch.

"Mom?" Emma said, her voice trembling. "Please."

"Go ahead and sit, honey. Let's talk this through."

"Can I just go to bed?"

"Sit down!" Roy hollered.

"Roy, please. Keep your voice down. The neighbors ..."

Emma walked away then, probably to go to her room, but Roy grabbed her by the left arm and spun her around. She cried out in pain and wobbled on her feet.

"Roy!" Tonya cried in horror. "Her arm is hurt!"

He grabbed Emma by her right arm and started dragging her. Emma screamed at the top of her lungs and braced her feet against his pulling, but he overpowered her and threw her onto the couch. She wasn't breathing. She looked terrified.

Tonya didn't know what to do. She was terrified too. Roy had never laid a hand on either of them.

"You sit down too!" he boomed.

She went to her daughter and put her arm around her shoulders. Maybe Emma was right. Maybe they should go somewhere. But where?

He sat down on the coffee table, so close to Emma that their knees were almost touching. "Start at the beginning."

Tonya could tell that he was trying to force himself to act calm, but he was failing. He was anything but calm. His fists and his jaw were clenched. His house of cards was falling all around him, and he was still trying to figure out how to stop it.

Emma's spine straightened, and she looked into his eyes. "Isabelle Martin, the meanest girl I've ever known, has been bullying me since Kindergarten—"

"I don't want to hear about Isabelle! Tell me where the accusations about Mrs. DeGrave are coming—"

"You told her to start at the beginning," Tonya said. Her voice had grown stronger. Was Emma's strength rubbing off on her? "So let her tell it."

Roy grimaced. This was the closest she'd come to talking back to him in years. "Fine." He looked at Emma.

"So even though you've refused to believe me that the Martins are evil, they are. And I got to hear ..." Emma's voice cracked. "Isabelle is a demon, so I got to hear from a *demon* that my *daddy* is a lying, cheating, gross pervert." She leaned forward, and her voice got louder. "I got to hear from the meanest girl alive that my father the pastor is nothing but a fake, nothing but a fraud, which means my whole life is one big lie, which means *God* is one big lie! And I want to thank you so much for letting me hear it from her, because, you know, it wouldn't have been painful enough to hear it from someone who doesn't hate me." Emma's face twisted up in anger. "And you know what? Mary Sue wasn't even *surprised* to hear it. So that means that everyone in the church knows, because Mary Sue is the last person to know anything, so if she knows something, that means everyone knows."

Roy's face fell. She knew him well enough to know that in that second, he knew he'd lost the fight. This was out now. He wouldn't be able to reel it back in.

"And so *I stole a bike.* Your good little pastor's kid stole a bike and then I crashed it because I was trying to kill myself, because I would rather be dead than be your daughter. But then I had a better idea. I drove to Mrs. DeGrave's house."

Roy reeled back from his daughter.

"And I pounded on their front door, and I woke their whole family up, and then I told Mr. DeGrave what you and his wife have been up to, and then I called Mrs. DeGrave a *slut* because that's what she is!"

The crack rang out before Tonya had even realized what was coming. As her daughter's head snapped to the side, she still had trouble processing what had just happened. Her husband had backhanded her daughter across the face. Her whole body shook. Surely that hadn't just happened. But it had because her daughter was running out the front door. She stood to go after her, but Roy grabbed her by the arm. She tried to yank her arm away, but he wouldn't let go.

"I'll go get her in a minute," he said. "We need to talk."

Chapter 17

Tonya

Tonya had been submitting to this man's every want and wish for so long that she struggled to do otherwise, even now. "I need to go after her. You just heard her say that she wants to kill herself."

"In a minute," he snapped. "She's not really going to hurt herself. She was just trying to make me angry."

She wasn't so sure. She'd never seen her daughter so upset, and that was *before* her father had slapped her.

"Tonya, I need to know that you're with me on this, and then we'll go get her."

"With you on what?" she cried.

"We need to *fix* this."

Tonya's thoughts were so jumbled, she couldn't even begin to think about fixing anything. She needed time to calm down, to process.

"It's time for damage control. I will admit everything. I will apologize to the congregation. And hopefully they won't fire me."

"Of course they'll fire you!"

He looked stunned, but he finally let go of her arm. "Not if you help me. Ask them not to. Ask them for mercy. It'll be good. It will show them that I'm human, that I struggle right along with them."

She almost snickered. How many years had he spent pretending that he *wasn't* human, that he *didn't* struggle right along with them?

"Think about the congregation. Think about the families. Where will they go?"

She didn't think they'd go anywhere. She thought they'd stay right where they were and find a new pastor. She realized he was trying to use her love for those families to control her. Well, the joke was on him, because she didn't even love most of them. Most of the time, she was faking it. Faking it for Jesus. Faking it for Roy. How could he not have noticed that? Did he even know her?

He saw that this tack wasn't working and shifted his sail. "Where will we go?" He held out his arms. "We are homeless without this parsonage! And no other church is going to hire me. No other church is going to give us another home!"

He squinted. He was studying her, trying to figure out how best to manipulate her.

She couldn't let him manipulate her. Not this time. But even as she had this thought, she wasn't sure she could stop it from happening. "I need to go get Emma."

He completely ignored her statement. "And it's not like you're going to support us. You don't have any employable skills."

And there it was. The low self-esteem card. And why wouldn't he play that card? It was the card that always worked. It was the card that had gotten her to marry him. Yes, she'd loved him way back then, but hadn't he also convinced her that he was the best she could do?

"Please, Tonya. Think this through. We only have two choices." He sounded annoyingly calm, as if he was being completely rational. Had he already thought all of this through? "We can either fight to fix this, or we can let it fall apart. Think about what that will look like. We'll lose my job. We'll lose our home. We'll get divorced, and we'll split custody. That means that for half the time, you won't have Emma. At all."

Her breath caught. Not have Emma? There was no way she could live like that. She tried to think. Was that really what would happen? And then who knew who he would find for his next wife? Did she want another woman anywhere near her daughter? Her chest was so tight she couldn't breathe. Her brain spun with fears, and she didn't know which were legitimate and which were lies. Or maybe none of them were lies. She wished she could rewind life twenty-four hours. If only she hadn't sent Emma to the Puddys. She could have gone on not knowing.

"And you'll be a single mom working a menial minimum wage job, so even when you have Emma, you'll never see her. You'll be miserable. Emma will be miserable. We can't let this happen to our daughter."

"Can I please go look for her?" Her voice broke.

"Tell me you'll help me fix this."

"Fine." She didn't know what else to say. She could never live with only fifty percent of Emma.

"Fine. Let's go find her."

She didn't want his help, but he followed her to the door anyway.

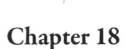

Chapter 18

Emma

Emma didn't know where to go. She had nowhere to go. She was too tired to go anywhere. She lay down on her lawn and looked at the sky. The lights from town prevented her from seeing most of the stars, and this made her even angrier. "Why, God? How? How could you let this happen? Are you even real?" She paused, waiting for him to answer, desperate for a sign, any sign, even something that she could pretend was a sign. But there was nothing. "You're not real, are you? It's all a lie? The Isabelles of the world are really in charge? And the weak people cluster around wooden crosses and get excited about heaven because this life stinks so bad? Is that the truth of the world?"

She heard a noise and rolled onto her side. Mrs. Patterson's porch light was on. That hadn't been on before, had it? Had she *ever* seen that light on before?

"What's your name?" a female voice called.

Emma squinted, trying to see its source. "Emma."

"Come on, Emma. Come on inside."

It wasn't until Mrs. Patterson's door closed that Emma realized it had been open an inch. Mrs. Patterson? She was inviting her into her house? Well, of course she was. This was the strangest evening of her life, so why wouldn't it get even stranger? She was tempted to accept the invitation, but she couldn't quite will her legs to work. But then she heard her parents coming—both of them—and she was on her feet and scurrying toward Mrs. Patterson's door.

When she reached it, there was no one there. She knocked softly.

"Come on in."

She slowly opened the door and stepped tentatively inside. The kitchen was dimly lit and smelled like molasses. Instantly, Emma felt welcome and safe. She shut the door behind her. "Do you mind if I turn off your porch light? I don't want my parents to find me."

A woman stepped out of the shadows. She was remarkably normal looking. She had short, neat hair and wore silky pajamas. She didn't look like a hermit or a psychopath or a witch. She wasn't nearly as old as Emma had imagined she would be. She gave Emma a tentative smile and reached past her to flick a switch. "There. You're hidden away, just like me."

Emma let out a long breath. "Thank you."

"Come on in. Have a seat. Tell me why you're lying in the middle of the lawn crying."

Emma followed her into a living room that was so welcoming she almost cried. Mrs. Patterson gestured toward a couch, and Emma gratefully sank into it. "I know you don't know me, but would you mind if I took a little nap here?"

"Of course not. Can I get you anything to eat or drink first? I'm all out of berry pie," she said with a twinkle in her eye, "but I've got some ginger snap cookies."

Emma hadn't thought she was hungry, but the mention of ginger snaps made her mouth water. "That would be awesome. Thank you."

"You want some milk to go with it?"

The mention of milk made Emma miss Mary Sue. She shouldn't have run off like that. She hoped Mary Sue didn't think she was mad at her. She hoped when this was all over that they could be real friends.

Would this ever be all over?

"Or hot chocolate?"

Emma realized she hadn't answered her about the milk.

"Sorry, I'm so tired that my brain's not really working. I would love some hot chocolate. Thank you."

"You betcha. Coming right up."

Emma woke up to the scent of ginger and sat up straight to take the plate from Mrs. Patterson's hands.

Mrs. Patterson set a steaming mug down on the small coffee table in front of her.

"Thank you for inviting me in. I really needed a place to hide. Things aren't so good at my house right now." She stopped talking. All her life she'd been so private about her family life. She'd been trained to be that way. As a pastor's family, they lived in a fishbowl. They had to keep their boundaries firm. But right now, she cared little about boundaries. Apparently, those had been lies too. She took a bite of cookie. It was delicious and made her feel better from head to toe. As she chewed, she realized that Mrs. Patterson might not know who she was. She swallowed and then hiked a thumb over her shoulder. "I live right next door."

"I know who you are. I'm not so insulated as people think."

"Do you ..." She realized she was about to be nosy and stopped herself.

"Go ahead and ask." Her smile was soft and sincere.

"Do you ever go out?"

She shook her head. "No need to."

Emma took another bite and then looked around the room. "You have a really nice house. It's ..." Again, she'd been on the verge of putting her foot in her mouth. She really had to get some sleep.

"You know what? You don't really know me, and I don't really know you, but let's decide right now to be friends. Deal?"

Emma giggled. "Sure."

"Sure. Good. And now that we're friends, let me tell you a little something about me. Do you know what pretenses are?"

Emma had heard the word, but she didn't dare try to define it. She shook her head and polished off the first cookie.

"A pretense is a false showing of something. It's playing make-believe. It's essentially lying. People do it all the time, but I don't. So right now, if you have a question you want to ask, go ahead and ask it. Don't tiptoe around pretending to be polite. You got something on your mind, just say it."

Emma was stunned. This was a very different worldview than the one that had been drilled into her head. *Everyone is watching. We must always be at the top of our game. We must never offend anyone.* Emma swallowed hard. "I had a thought, and at first it was a compliment, but then I realized it kind of wasn't."

Mrs. Patterson nodded. "You were going to say that my house is much nicer on the inside than the outside."

Emma nodded.

"Go ahead and eat your other cookie. You're absolutely right. It's hard to keep up with the outside of a house when you never go outside. I pay people to mow, rake, and shovel, but that's about all I manage for outside maintenance."

Emma busied herself with her cookie.

"And now you're wondering why I never go outside?"

Emma gave her a small nod.

"So go ahead and ask."

She swallowed. "Why don't you ever go outside?"

"And now I will not worry about offending you and tell you that *that* is none of your business!" She tittered. "Finish your cookie. You're welcome to get some sleep, but we should probably tell your parents you're safe. I'm sure your mother is worried sick."

Emma didn't miss the fact that she'd said "your mother," not "your parents" or "your father." Was that a coincidence, or did even the recluse neighbor know more about Emma's life than Emma did? "I don't want to leave," Emma said. "If you don't mind, I feel so safe here. And I am so tired. But you're right. I don't want to scare my mother." She reached for her back pocket, unsure if her phone would still be there. It was. "I'll call her."

Chapter 19

Tonya

Tonya was certain that she was going to throw up. She was hiding in the top of the stairwell, only steps away from the pulpit where she would soon wave her dirty laundry around for all to see. She could hear the congregation filling the sanctuary, but they were quieter than usual. Was there a heaviness in the air, or was that just her? Surely everyone had heard by now. Surely everyone in the sanctuary knew everything there was to know.

She straightened her skirt and fluffed her hair. She'd done her best with her makeup, but she knew her eyes were still red and puffy. She had managed to get a few hours of sleep after Emma had called, but those hours had been fitful.

Her husband appeared in the stairwell below her, and she fantasized about kicking him in the chest and watching him tumble butt over teakettle back down the stairs. But she didn't do that, of course. Instead, she stood perfectly still and stayed quiet.

He paused beside her. "You ready?"

Of course not. How could she ever be ready for this? She nodded.

"All right. Let's get this done." He opened the door so that everyone could see them, and she thought she might pass out. He took her hand and led her to the front of the room. She'd expected them to go up on the platform and get behind the pulpit, but that's not where they went. They stood in front of everyone on the floor level, and she realized this was part of his humility act.

Tonya scanned the room for Alexis's face. She didn't know what she'd do if she saw it. She wasn't even sure she'd be able to handle the sight of her. But she wasn't there. Of course she wasn't. What kind of a woman would show up in public to be embarrassed like that?

Roy cleared his throat. "Good morn—" He stopped and gave the sound booth a scolding stare. One of them fiddled with something and then gave him a thumbs up.

Tonya wanted to rip her hand out of his sweaty clutch and run screaming from the building. She wanted to rip off her stupid pencil skirt and never put on pantyhose again. She wanted to wipe her makeup off and never look at a lipstick again. Instead, she found a child's face in the crowd and forced a smile. This was a trick she'd learned years ago. Always easier to smile at children.

"Good morning," her husband said again. He let out a long sigh. "Welcome, everyone. I don't see any new faces, which, for the first time ever, is probably a good thing. This won't be a great day for visitors. I'm so grateful that I'm standing in front of my family—" His voice cracked on the word family, and Tonya knew that this crack was one hundred percent disingenuous.

As he'd faked falling apart, he also faked pulling it together.

Tonya pulled her hand from his. She couldn't bear to touch him. She felt him stiffen in anger at this, but too bad. "Today is the hardest day of my life. I've spent all night in prayer, and I stand before you now a humble and broken man. I have sinned. I am chief of sinners."

Oh, of course. Subtly compare yourself to Paul.

"I have sinned against my wife, against my family, and against you all. I have repented, and now I ask your forgiveness. I fell into temptation, but just like King David with Bathsheba, I have come out of this a man after God's own heart."

Absolutely. Compare yourself to the King of Israel. And you haven't come out of anything yet.

"My wonderful wife has leaned on the strength of the Lord in order to forgive me in the great tradition of Sarah."

Brilliant. Compare me to Sarah, and by doing so you get to be Abraham. And I haven't forgiven you. You haven't even apologized.

"We're going to have some worship music in a minute, and then I've asked Brother Bart to preach today. I ask you all to seek God and to forgive me. I am only a man, and I've made a mistake, but I am repentant"—

Yeah, you already said that.

—"and I am more motivated than ever to serve God and to serve you all. I love you."

When was the last time you told me you loved me? It's been years. And did you even mean it when you said it?

She noticed Jason DeGrave leaning against the back wall of the sanctuary with his arms folded across his chest. He hardly ever came to church with his mother, and Tonya might not have even recognized him except that she knew him from all his sports heroism. When their eyes met, he offered her a small, sincere, slightly sad smile, and she tried to return it but wasn't sure her tired face had managed.

Then he dropped his arms and turned to leave the sanctuary. And she wished she could follow him.

Chapter 20

Esther

Esther was on her knees in front of the altar. She didn't know how long she'd been there and had stopped praying a while ago but had lingered in the peace of it.

She hadn't realized anyone else had entered the church until Rachel said, "I can't believe you can still get on your knees."

Esther jumped and then started to pull herself to her feet.

"Or you can get down, but can you get back up?" Rachel stepped closer. "Do you need a hand?"

"No, I can do it." She came to a wobbly stand. "What brings you here?"

Rachel shrugged. "It's Sunday morning. I don't have a church. I figured I'd come here and pray."

Esther smiled. "Great minds think alike. Don't let me stop you." She gestured toward the altar.

"No thanks. These knees have done some hard living. I can pray in a pew."

The door opened, and Barbara and Cathy came inside. "Well, hello ladies!" Cathy said.

"Good morning," Esther and Rachel replied in unison.

"Just couldn't stay away, huh?" Cathy sang out.

Barbara looked around. "Wow, it's looking better already."

"It's amazing what a little Pine-Sol can accomplish," Esther said.

"Indeed! Well," Cathy said, "we thought we'd come pray for a while. Then we're going out to lunch. You want to join us?"

They both agreed and were arguing about which restaurant they would patronize when Dawn and Vera came in. "Did someone invite you?" Dawn cried, obviously worried she'd missed an invitation.

"No one other than the Holy Spirit," Esther said quickly.

Dawn's face relaxed. "Oh good."

Barbara looked around. "Vicky is going to have a fit that we're all here and she's not. Should we call her?"

"You don't need to," Esther said as Vicky walked in.

"What are you all doing here?" Vicky said accusingly.

"Good morning to you too," Esther said. "We're going to pray."

"All right then. Wait for me."

The ladies settled into the front pews.

"Nice hat," Vicky said to Rachel.

Esther flinched. Vicky's sarcasm sounded especially harsh in their new sanctuary.

"You've always been jealous of my hat collection," Rachel said with her tongue in her cheek.

Rachel had an extensive collection of ridiculous hats straight out of the seventies. While Esther had never been jealous of the hats themselves, she'd often envied Rachel's nerve. The hats often clashed with the chunky beads she wore around her neck, making the hats appear even more brassy.

Esther was prone to elastic-waist navy blue pants and light blue t-shirts. *Boring.*

Vicky rolled her eyes at Rachel and then looked at Esther. "Are we praying aloud or silently?"

"Either, or, or both," Dawn said.

"Fine," Vicky said, and then began to pray aloud. "Father in heaven, I pray for this building. I pray you will sanctify it and bless it. It seems you have called seven old broads to get these pistons firing again, so you'd better equip us to do so because we're all running a little low on fuel."

Esther snickered. *There* was the Vicky she knew and loved.

"I pray for this neighborhood. I pray we can make a difference. I pray you show us how to make a difference. I pray you get people through the doors, but also give us the ability and the courage to go out through the doors and reach people outside. If there are needs, use us to meet them." She laughed. "Oh, what am I saying? Of course there are needs, so use us to meet them. Use this building. Use these women. Use the gifts we have, those we know about and those we don't yet. If Cathy is meant to preach, then you'd better help her do so. I've got my reservations about that one, Lord, but you are in charge."

Esther resisted the urge to peek at Cathy.

"I pray you protect this property from those who don't want us to succeed, from those who don't want *you* to succeed. And please send us some young blood to help us fix the place up. We ask you for a new wheelchair ramp. We ask you for a new furnace and the fuel to fill it. We ask you to help Alex fix the plumbing and help Kyle fix everything else. We ask you for money to pay Kyle, although it would be even better if you could convince him to work for free."

Esther could almost hear Kyle's mother rolling her eyes.

"I pray that you help us find windows. I'd prefer they be stained-glass, but that might be complicated, but at least get us windows, Lord. Windows to let that beautiful sunlight in. Windows to let people look inside and see this beautiful sanctuary. I pray for flowers in the flowerbeds and children in the Sunday school rooms. And most of all, God, I ask you to take charge of this ridiculous project. Don't let us get in the way. Have your will done here, Lord, or all of this is for nothing. We want all of the glory to go to you and you alone." She took a deep breath. "And all of his people said ..."

"Amen."

Chapter 21

Tonya

"I'm going in after her," Roy announced.

They were sitting at their kitchen table looking at their lunch.

"And how do you plan to do that?" Tonya asked.

"I'm going to knock on her door and then go in and get our daughter."

"Mrs. Patterson doesn't open the door."

"She certainly did for our daughter!"

"Yes, she did. And isn't that interesting?" Tonya had been wondering about that. How had that gone down? Had her daughter been desperate enough to knock on Mrs. Patterson's door? And if so, Mrs. Patterson must have sensed her desperation in order to not only open the door but invite her in? Tonya could hardly believe that Emma had spent the night there. And yet, she was fairly comfortable with it. Emma was safe and she was close-by. And she wasn't trapped in this house having to deal with the fallout of her father's mess.

"Maybe we should call the police."

She hated the sound of that. She didn't want to complicate Mrs. Patterson's life simply because the woman had been kind to her daughter. But how to convince her husband of that?

"That would only embarrass ..." She'd almost said "you" but she caught herself in time and said "us" instead. "She hasn't committed any crime, and the police would just laugh at us."

Roy groaned. "You're probably right." He put his head in his hands. "Why haven't they called yet?"

The elders. This was what he was really upset about. He was only trying to distract himself with his daughter's whereabouts.

"It's only been an hour."

He looked at the clock. "An hour and a half."

Fine. Whatever.

"Did you notice that the Puddys weren't in church?"

She had indeed noticed that, but she hadn't been surprised. Why would they want their family to go sit under an adulterer pastor? Why would any family want that?

"That doesn't look very good."

"I doubt anyone even knows they were a part of it."

He gave her a pitying look. "You are so naive. Everyone knows all of it."

She had so many questions she wanted to ask him, and this was her chance. He was right there in front of her, waiting for the phone to ring. And yet she couldn't quite muster the courage.

Suddenly, he slapped the table and stood up. "I'm going to get her."

"Wait!"

He stopped and looked down at her. "What?"

Ask him. Do it for Emma. Distract him. Her thoughts chased one another around in a sickening game of tag. Which question to ask and how to phrase it?

He turned toward the door.

"Isabelle and Mary Sue knew," she spat out. "Did you know that people knew?"

Slowly, he turned back toward her. "What did you say?"

His anger emboldened her. Or maybe it was the lack of justification for that anger. "You're worried about how it looks to people that the Puddys weren't in church. But one of the Puddy children knew you were having an affair. And so did Isabelle." He opened his mouth to argue, but she talked louder and faster. "There's no way two children were the only ones to know, so others must have. I'm asking you if you knew they knew?"

"Of course not," he spat out. "If I'd known they knew, I would've stopped it." His face jerked as if he'd been slapped by his own words. This was the closest he'd come to admitting the truth, that he'd knowingly, strategically, deceitfully carried on with a married woman.

"Where did you do it?" she quietly asked.

"Tonya, don't do this."

"Where?"

"Where what?"

"Where did you have your affair?"

"Oh, stop calling it an affair! You make it sound like it was some long drawn-out romantic—" Again, he caught himself.

"If it wasn't a romance, then what was it?"

"It was just sex!" he said too loudly. "Men have needs!"

He'd done it again. Turned the tables. Made it her fault. She wasn't sexual enough for him. He had "needs." He'd had to go elsewhere to get those needs met.

This trick wasn't going to work this time. She knew this wasn't her fault. "Don't talk to me about needs."

His eyes widened. He hadn't been expecting that.

"Where did you do it?" she asked again. Her voice had a sharp edge to it.

His face twisted up, and he suddenly looked reptilian. "I'm not going to answer that question. So stop asking it."

"Do you love her?"

His laughter answered her. She expected this to be a relief. She thought this would be good news to hear that he didn't really care about Alexis, but it wasn't a relief and it didn't feel like good news. It felt like nothing. It didn't matter whether he loved Alexis. "I don't know if I can do this," she said quietly.

He looked at the phone. "Wait to hear from the elders. If they fire me, you can leave. I'll help you pack."

"And if they don't fire you, I can't leave? Is that what you're saying?"

He looked up at her. "I thought we already agreed on this?"

What had she agreed to, exactly? She couldn't remember. She was confused, and her confusion made her angry. Her heart ached for Emma, for the comfort of her presence.

The phone rang.

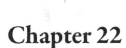

Chapter 22

Emma

Emma just happened to be looking out Mrs. Patterson's kitchen window when she saw what looked like Jason DeGrave in her driveway.

"I think I have to go outside," Emma said mostly to herself.

Mrs. Patterson stepped up beside her. "I rarely find that to be true."

Emma giggled at her phrasing. "I think that's Jason DeGrave in front of my house."

"Who's Jason DeGrave?"

"He's a straight-A superstar jock and he's the son of the woman my dad is sleeping with."

"Oh, I see. And from the sound of your voice, this Jason DeGrave is also quite handsome?"

"Yes, but that has nothing to do with anything. He's in high school."

"Oh, posh. In a few years, you'll both be paying taxes, just like the rest of us."

Emma gasped. "He just went into my house. This can't be good. I have to go." She looked at Mrs. Patterson worriedly. "I'm sorry. I don't want to leave you."

She tittered. "That's all right. You do what you have to do."

"Can I come back?" She thought that maybe, if Mrs. Patterson said no, she might stay put and let Jason DeGrave fend for himself.

But Mrs. Patterson said, "Of course. Just don't bring friends or family."

"Deal." She had an urge to hug the woman and after a few seconds of hemming and hawing, decided to follow the urge.

Mrs. Patterson stiffened under Emma's embrace, and Emma released her promptly. "Thank you for everything." She stepped out of the house and closed the door behind her. Did she really want to leave? Mrs. Patterson's house was so safe. The world outside her walls was the opposite of safe. But why had Jason DeGrave just walked into her house? She heard her mother scream and took off across the lawn at a dead run.

She found Jason in her living room, straddling her father, who was on his back on the floor. Her father had his hands over his face in a pathetic attempt to ward off the much younger man's blows. Jason's left hand had a fistful of her father's shirt, and his right hand was drawn back, ready to deliver a blow to her father's face. From the looks of things, it wouldn't be the first blow.

"Jason, no!" she cried and hurried across the room.

Her mother stood against the wall, whimpering helplessly.

Jason either didn't hear her plea or ignored it and punched her father in the face. Her father made a weird gurgling sound as Jason brought his fist back up again.

Emma leapt onto Jason's back, her right arm going up over his raised one and pulling it partly down.

He reared back as if trying to buck her off; at the same time, he looked over his shoulder and saw it was her. "Emma?" His whole body relaxed. They toppled backward in a tangle of limbs, and he did his best not to crush her. Breathing heavily, he got himself to his feet and then held out a hand toward her. She took it, and he effortlessly pulled her to her feet. She brushed off the seat of her shorts, suddenly feeling self-conscious. She was still wearing the same clothes she'd rolled around in the ditch in.

"What happened to you?" he asked, managing to sound concerned.

"My father happened to me." She looked down at the pathetic man who had rolled onto his side.

"Call the police," he sputtered, and no one moved.

"Yeah, your father happened to me too."

Her mother pointed at the door. "Get out of here before I call the police!"

"Call them!" her father tried to order, but his directive had no legs.

"Mom," Emma said, embarrassed, "Jason has every right to be angry."

"He doesn't have the right to assault someone! Get out of my house!"

"Mom! Please!"

Her mother turned her fiery eyes on Emma. "It's not like his mother is innocent! It takes two to tango!"

Emma found this phrase deeply embarrassing.

Jason held both hands up. "I'll leave. But I'm not angry because he had an affair with my mother. I'm angry that he's made her out to be a whore that dragged him into the darkness. Do you know what people are saying? That my mother ruined the good pastor! Are you kidding me?" He looked down at the man on the floor, who was trying to sit up. "There is no good pastor here." He pointed at her father. "Stop talking trash about my mother. She's a good woman." He looked at Emma. "I'm sorry, Emma." He started toward the door.

"I'm calling the police!" her father called after him.

She followed Jason out through the door and watched him climb into his car. "Hey."

Jason looked at her expectantly.

"I'm sorry too."

He nodded. "I think everyone is. Everyone except the good pastor."

Chapter 23

Fiona

F iona Patterson watched the two young people in the pastor's driveway. She'd guessed correctly. The DeGrave boy was indeed handsome.

Emma wasn't coming back.

How foolish she had been to think otherwise. She was furious with herself. She knew better, had known better for years. For more than a decade, she had taken care of herself, kept herself safe—so why had she recklessly flung open her door to that child?

Because she was a child. And because she'd been in need. *Be gentle with yourself,* Fiona told herself. *You're not a monster. You still have a heart. That's why you opened your door.* And now she was paying the price.

The DeGrave boy started his car and drove away. Emma looked in her direction, and Fiona jumped back, letting the curtain fall shut. Tears burned her eyes. It had been fun having a friend for a few hours.

Chapter 24

Emma

Emma watched Jason DeGrave drive away and then wondered what to do next. She looked longingly at Mrs. Patterson's house and saw a curtain fall shut. She could simply go back there. She turned and looked at her own front door. Or she could go make sure her parents were okay.

Did she even care about that, though? Her mother would probably be okay, and her father had deserved what he'd gotten.

Oh no! The police! She had to stop him from having Jason arrested. She ran inside, but he was already on his phone. He stood leaning on the piano with his cell pressed to his ear.

"Who's he calling?" she asked her mother, even though she knew the answer.

"The police."

"Dad, stop!"

He ignored her.

She went closer to him. "Dad, please, can we just talk about this first?"

He gave her a patronizing look. "There's nothing to talk about." Apparently, he was taken off hold because he spoke rapidly into the phone.

She reached for it, desperate to stop him. "Dad!"

He pushed her away, and her mother grabbed her from behind. "Emma! Stop! What are you thinking?"

She whirled on her mother. "What am *I* thinking? What are *you* thinking? Why are you still standing in this house?"

Her face fell. "Honey, it's complicated." She reached out to gently swipe Emma's hair off her face, but Emma shrank away from her touch.

"Don't touch me." The look on her mother's face brought instant guilt to Emma's heart. She tried to ignore it. Glaring at her father, she said, "Mom, please. Let's go. I know Mrs. Patterson will let you stay there until we figure out a plan."

Her mother took a deep breath. "The elders called. They're not firing your fath—"

"The elders?" Emma screeched. "You think I care about *the elders*? That's the last thing I'm worried about!"

"I know, but listen. Think of the church. Your father is still the pastor."

Emma put her hands on her hips and tried to calm down. She wanted to figure out what was happening, and she couldn't do that if she was hysterical.

Her mother mistook this forced calm for interest in her father's pastoral career. "They've asked him to take two months of leave. We can still live here. We will still go to church. But he will take the time to seek God."

Emma rolled her eyes. "Mom, I don't *want* to live here." She held her hands out to her sides and looked around. "This whole house is a sham. Our life is a sham." She leveled a gaze. "Our family is a sham. Your *marriage* is a sham."

The words didn't create quite the slap Emma had anticipated.

Her father hung up the phone. "We need to talk, Emma."

She looked at him. Part of her wanted to run away. Part of her was curious about what nonsense he was about to spew.

"Please, have a seat."

"No thank you." Part of her wanted him to throw her onto the couch again. Then maybe she'd be the one calling the cops.

He took a long breath. He looked irritated that he had to be dealing with her. Hadn't he loved her when she was little? Was she misremembering that?

"Your father is human, Emma, and I made a mistake. But we need to work together to get through this. We can't have you hiding out at the neighbor's house."

For a few seconds, she had no words. Then, "I'm not hiding out."

"Whatever you're doing, you need to be here with us."

"You just called the cops on a *kid*. A kid whose life you just ruined."

"Oh, please. I didn't ruin anything."

"Are you kidding me? He's like a local celebrity, and now you've made his mother out to be a whore!"

"I didn't *make* his mother do anything."

Her mother flinched. "Could we please not talk about Mrs. DeGrave?"

Emma narrowed her eyes. She was angry that her father wasn't in more pain. Why wasn't he in more pain? Why was everyone else suffering because of what he'd done, but he'd gotten off with only a black eye and a bloody lip? Practically scot-free. "Are you going to keep seeing her?"

"What? Of course not."

Emma sneaked a glance at her mother. She didn't look convinced.

"Was she the only one?"

He hesitated. "Of course."

"Why would we believe you?"

"Because I'm telling the truth."

Emma laughed coldly. "Sure you are." She felt so powerless. She didn't know if he was lying. She didn't know anything. "If you're going to press charges on Jason, then I'm moving in with Mrs. Patterson."

"You can't *move in* with anyone. You're a kid."

"Then I'll get emaciated."

Her father barked out a laugh. "You mean *emancipated*?"

Her cheeks grew hot, and she fought back tears.

"Because emaciated means you're starving. But you're not that far off, because you will starve if we don't feed you. And don't tell me that Mrs. Patterson will feed you. She can barely take care of herself and she'll grow tired of you soon enough."

"Like you?" Emma spat. "Like you've grown tired of me?"

He looked surprised. "You know what I'm tired of? I'm tired of you acting like a spoiled little brat! None of this has anything to do with you!"

His words were like ice water to her face. She couldn't believe he'd just said that. She looked at her mother. "I love you, Mom. I'm going to go check on Jason."

She slammed the door so hard that the house shook. Only then did she wish she'd grabbed some clothes and supplies.

She would sneak in later. Right now, she had to get to Jason.

Chapter 25

Emma

She was too late. The police were already in Jason's driveway. A few people lingered on the sidewalk, watching them. She started walking faster and by the time she got to the driveway, a policeman was bringing Jason out of the house. His hands were handcuffed behind his back.

"Wait!" she cried and then felt foolish. What was she going to say next? What could she do?

The policeman looked at her, not unkindly.

"It's not his fault," she said lamely.

His father stood in the doorway of the house, looking furious.

"Jason," she said, feeling frantic, "tell me what to do!"

He shook his head. "I don't know." The fear in his voice terrified her. This was big, tough Jason DeGrave. He was fearless on the field and on the court. He ruled the high school hallways. He'd been so brave when he'd pounded her father's face in. Now he sounded like a scared little kid.

She looked at his father. "What do we do?"

"*We* don't do anything. I told him not to go over there, and he didn't listen. As usual." He slammed the door shut.

The policeman put Jason in the car and shut the door. Then he looked at her. "We're taking him to the county jail. If someone posts bail, he will be released. And he'll need a lawyer."

She nodded, her throat too dry to speak. How was she going to post bail? She had no money. And she didn't know any lawyers. She watched them drive away and then started walking. She needed to talk to her mother, but she really couldn't. Firstly, her mother was standing right beside her father, and secondly, whose side was her mother even on? She'd seemed happy that Jason would be arrested.

Emma felt sick. She cut across a few backyards and then followed Mrs. Patterson's fence to the front of her house.

Mrs. Patterson answered on the second knock. She looked surprised to see her. "Come on in."

Emma followed her through the kitchen and into the living room.

"I saw you talking to the jock." She sat down in her armchair. "How did that go?"

"Not good. He beat my father up, and now he's been arrested."

A smile played on the older woman's lips. Her eyes were red. Had she been crying? "He beat your father up?"

"Are you okay?"

She nodded quickly. "Of course. He beat your father up?" she asked again.

"He sure did. That part wasn't so bad. But it was made worse, I think, by the fact that my father didn't fight back. I don't know if it was because he doesn't know how to fight or if he didn't want to hit a kid, but—"

"Are you sure that boy is a kid?"

"What do you mean?"

"I mean that, if he is eighteen or older, he might be in a lot of trouble."

"He's going to be a junior, so I don't think he's eighteen yet, but I still think he's in a lot of trouble. Do you have any idea how this stuff works? I need to help him. The policeman said that if someone posted bail, then Jason would be released and that he would need a lawyer. But I don't have bail and I don't know any lawyers."

"If I were you, I wouldn't get involved." She wouldn't look at her. She stared at the television, which was on mute.

"What? I'm already involved."

"Not really. Not with this part. That boy made a decision, and there will be consequences."

"But it wasn't his fault!" How was it that no adult could see that?

"Don't be ridiculous. His mother did a stupid thing. No one held a gun to his head and made him do a different stupid thing."

What? She'd thought Mrs. Patterson was on her side. "But he was so angry at my father!"

"Yes, he was. And he has a right to be angry. But he doesn't have a right to go assault someone."

Emma tipped her head back to keep more tears from falling. She was so tired of crying. She needed less crying and more action. Everything was spiraling out of control, and she needed to find some part of this mess, some small part, that she could fix. But she didn't think she could do it alone. She needed Mrs. Patterson's help. But how to convince her?

"Why did you open the door for Raven?"

"Who?"

Emma looked at her. "My jerk friend. A few days ago, she knocked on your door and then ran away?"

Mrs. Patterson looked down at her hands. "Oh, that."

"Yes. Why did you open the door?"

She hesitated. "Because she looked scared."

"And me?"

"What about you?"

"Why did you see me all pathetic, crying on my lawn and invite me into your house?"

"Because," she muttered, "you were also scared."

Emma leaned forward. "Jason is a kid. And he is scared. I'll admit that I don't know him that well, but I know he's not a bad person. He's not violent. He's not evil. He's really smart and he's got a bright future ahead of him, but right now, he's just a scared kid." She paused. "And he's in *jail*. I doubt he's ever been in trouble in his life, and now he's in a grown-up jail."

Mrs. Patterson let out a long sigh. "How much is his bail?"

"I have no idea."

"Hmm..." She looked contemplative. "We could call the jail and find out, but you'd have to do it. I don't talk on the phone."

"You don't talk on the phone?" Her mother spent most of her life on the phone.

She shook her head. "Sure don't. I wouldn't even have one but I'm worried the house might catch fire. Won't his folks post bail?"

"I don't know. His father didn't seem to care, but I don't know if his mother will do something."

"So you should call her. She might already be on her way to the jail. If she's not, which I find hard to believe, *then* you can call the jail and ask them how much bail is."

"You want me to call the woman who slept with my father?"

Mrs. Patterson shrugged. "Do you want to get your Jason out of jail?"

Emma narrowed her eyes. "He's not *my* Jason, and stop trying to make this out to be a crush thing. It's not. I don't think of him in that way."

"If you say so. Either way, if you want to help him, the first step is to call his mother."

Chapter 26

Emma

Emma wasn't sure of the best way to get her father's mistress's phone number. She couldn't believe God had tasked her with such a mission. Her first thought was to check her father's cell phone, but if he'd been sneaking around, would he keep her phone number in his phone? Or would it be listed under some code name? Thinking about this made her sick to her stomach. Then she considered the church directory. That would likely have some phone number for Alexis DeGrave, but would it be her cell? Or her home phone? Her husband never went to church, so maybe it would be her cell. But Emma wasn't willing to bet on it, and she didn't really want to speak to that man again. Maybe she should just dial whatever number she found and then if a man answered, hang up.

Neither of these plans were great, but they both required her leaving Mrs. Patterson's house. When she shared this realization, Mrs. Patterson looked sad.

"I'll be right back."

She nodded, but she still looked sad.

Emma had another thought. "Do you need anything? While I'm out?"

"Need anything?" she repeated. "What would I need?"

Emma looked around the house and shrugged. "I don't know, but if you don't go out, I thought maybe there might be something you wanted that you can't get."

Her back straightened, and she lifted her chin. "I have everything I need, thank you."

Emma hesitated. "How do you get what you need? How do you get food?"

She smiled. "Child, you need to see my garden."

Emma was surprised. Garden? It was true that a tall fence surrounded Mrs. Patterson's entire backyard, but it had never occurred to Emma that she was back there gardening. So she *did* go outside. It was a relief to hear this. She left her house. She just didn't leave her property.

"What about other things? Meat? Toilet paper? Toothpaste?"

She chuckled and started shooing her toward the door. "Anything I can't grow myself, I have shipped."

They'd reached the front door. Emma couldn't remember a world without the internet, but she knew there had been one. "What about before?"

She stopped walking and furrowed her brow. "Before what?"

"Before you could have stuff delivered?"

Her voice softened. "I haven't always been like this. I used to be young and out and about, just like you." She opened the door.

Emma wanted to ask her what had changed. Why had *she* changed? But she also needed to get to Jason. "I'll be back," she said again.

Mrs. Patterson nodded again.

"And then I'd love to see your garden."

Mrs. Patterson smiled, but it didn't reach her eyes.

As Emma crossed Mrs. Patterson's front lawn and then her own, her curiosity about her mysterious neighbor faded as a feeling of dread grew. She so didn't want to talk to this woman, but Mrs. Patterson was right. If Jason was already being bailed out, she could stop freaking out about it.

Her mother was lying on the couch but sat up abruptly when she came in. "You came back?"

Why was everyone so surprised by her appearances?

"Not for long," she said, wanting to hurt her mother.

It worked. Her face fell, and Emma felt ill with guilt. "I'm sorry, Mom. I'm not mad at you, and I don't want to hurt your feelings. Will you please just come with me?"

She hesitated, seeming to consider it. This encouraged Emma greatly.

"Emma, can we have an adult conversation?" She patted the seat beside her.

"Not right now. I have to figure out how to bail Jason out of jail."

She raised an eyebrow. "*You're* going to bail him out? With what money?"

"Well, first I was going to call Alexis and ask her to do it."

Her mother went pale. "I don't want you talking to that woman!"

"I don't want to talk to her either, Mom. I think I'm angrier with her than you are. But I need to help Jason. So do you want to help me bail him out? Because if not, I have to call Alexis."

"I'm not going to help. Think of how that would look. And stop calling Mrs. DeGrave by her first name. You need to call adults by their proper names. You know that."

Emma couldn't believe that her mother was worried about such things under the circumstances. And she could think of several adults who didn't deserve the respect of being called by their proper names. "I don't think Alexis is much of a wife to Mr. DeGrave."

Her mother sighed. She looked exhausted. She patted the seat again. "It's going to take forever to process Jason. Have a seat for just a minute."

Emma was overcome then by a desire for her mother, and she went to her quickly. She sat and buried her head in her chest and let the tears come. "Mom," she said, her voice muffled. "What a mess!"

Her mother squeezed her tightly and rubbed her back. "I know, honey. Don't I know it."

Emma leaned back and looked into her eyes. "Then let's *do* something about it! Let's pack a bag right now."

"That's the adult part of the conversation, Emma. You are young, and I've always tried to protect you from adult junk. I don't want to weigh down your spirit or your heart with the things adults have to worry about, but I feel like I might need to do that in this case, because none of this is as simple as you think it is."

"Mom, this is *so* simple." She was surprised at how convincing—how *adult-like*—her voice sounded.

A tear escaped her mother's eye, and she wiped it away. "Divorce is so messy, Emma. And child custody makes it even messier. Imagine a life where I only had you half the time. I can't live like that."

"That's what you're worried about?" Emma screeched. "Mom! I'm *thirteen*! I can decide who I live with and I choose you! Are you crazy?"

She shook her head. "I don't think you'll have a choice."

"That is not true! Mom, I *will* have a choice! I know lots of kids with divorced parents, and they all have a say in where they go. Maybe not when they were little, but they do now. Dad can't *make* me stay with him, ever." She grabbed her mother's hands and squeezed, desperate to convince her. "Mom, I choose *you*. I always choose *you*."

Chapter 27

Tonya

Tonya was speechless. Was her daughter correct? Because if so, that meant Roy had been wrong.

Had Roy been mistaken? Or had he lied? He knew how much she loved Emma. Had he tried to use that to his advantage?

She'd never be able to prove it, and yet she knew it was true.

This knowledge changed everything.

Could she be a divorced single mom? What would that look like? Fear took over her whole body. She had to fight to draw breath. "How would we live, Emma? I don't have a job."

"You get a job!" Emma cried. "Lots of people get jobs, Mom! I'll get a job! We can get help from the government!"

Tonya ripped her hands away from Emma's. "I will never do that!"

Emma rolled her eyes. "You'd rather stay with a man who cheats on you and throws your daughter onto the couch?"

Tonya scowled. "Don't act like your father abuses you. That was the first time he's ever touched you. This is all very hard and very scary for him too."

Emma groaned. "You can't seriously be feeling sorry for him right now."

No, she hadn't been. Not at all. So why was she trying to get her daughter to feel sorry for him?

She didn't know the answer to that.

"Fine. We won't get government help. So we get help from the church."

"What church?" her mother cried so loudly that Emma looked around.

"Where is Dad?"

"He went to the hospital."

"Alone? You didn't go with him?"

"He didn't want me to." Of course not. He'd probably picked up Alexis on the way so that she wouldn't bail her son out. Roy Mendell: beloved pastor; manipulator extraordinaire.

"Mom, *our* church. I know our church has helped families before. I know it's supposed to be all private, but kids talk. I know we buy heat and groceries for people all the time."

"But if we left, it wouldn't be our church anymore."

"So we find a different church!" Emma appeared to be thrilled by this idea.

How was it that she, the adult in the conversation, was so efficiently failing at having an adult conversation?

Emma slid closer to her and forced eye contact. "Mom, you can do this. We get a small, cheap apartment. We find a new church. You get a job. You are smart. You can do anything."

"But what about the church?" she said, ashamed of how weak she sounded.

"Mom, what about them? Dad created this mess, not you. And half the people are going to leave the church anyway." She stood up.

Tonya looked up at her. "What did you just say?"

"You heard me."

"But why do you say that?"

Emma folded her slender arms across her chest. "Because if I had my kids in a church where the pastor slept with some woman in the church, I would be going church shopping." She turned away from her mother and walked toward the kitchen. "Where's the church directory?"

"In the top desk drawer, but Emma, please don't call Alexis."

Chapter 28

Emma

Her mother hadn't called the woman Mrs. DeGrave—this gave Emma enormous satisfaction. It could have been a mistake, but Emma didn't think so. Her mother was frazzled, but she always called adults by their proper name when she talked to Emma.

Emma realized her mother was waiting for her to respond. "Mrs. Patterson said she wouldn't help me bail him out unless I made sure Alexis wasn't going to do it."

Her mother stood up and put her hand on her head. "Emma, stop! You don't need to bail anyone out! You're being ridiculous! He beat someone up! He beat up a *pastor*! He deserves to be in jail! And don't you take advantage of an elderly woman's loneliness by letting her spend money to bail Jason DeGrave out of that jail!"

"But she'll get the money back when he shows up in court!"

"Stop acting like you know everything!" She was shouting now. Apparently, the adult portion of their conversation was over. "She won't get the money back because it will all go straight to his fine! So unless he pays her back, she won't get paid back, and I highly doubt that thug is going to pay her back!"

"He's not a thug!" Emma screamed back. She ripped the drawer open with such force that it came out of the desk. She snatched the directory and then let the wooden drawer crash to the floor.

"Emma!" her mother screamed. "You're acting like a brat!"

Her mother sounded like she was stark raving mad. Emma realized she did not want to look like that, so she forced herself to calm down. Levelly, she said, "So are you."

She didn't know if it was her forced calm or the words themselves, but her comment didn't land well. Her mother's face drained. "Don't you dare talk to me like that!" Her ashen skin made Emma feel guilty, but at least she wasn't screaming anymore.

"Mom, I love you. I don't want to fight with you. I just don't understand how you're thinking any of this. I don't understand how you're on Dad's side." She started toward the door. "Let me know if you change your mind. I'm going back to Mrs. Patterson's."

She hoped her mother would follow her or at least tell her to wait, but her mother did nothing. What was wrong with her? If someone had asked Emma a week ago how much her mother loved her father, she would have shrugged and said, "Not much?" Had she had it all wrong? And if it wasn't love keeping her mother in that house, then what was it? It couldn't be the fear of losing Emma because Emma had promised she wouldn't let that happen.

She didn't have to knock this time. Mrs. Patterson opened the door before she even got there. "Did you call?"

"Not yet. I had to get out of the house. But I've got the number." At least, she had the directory; she *hoped* she also had the number. She flipped through the heavily photocopied pages until she got to the Ds. Sure enough, there was Alexis DeGrave. Her stomach turned. She took her phone out. She had to hurry up and do this before she lost her nerve. She dialed the number and waited.

"Hello?" a tired voice answered.

"Mrs. DeGrave?" She defaulted to the formal name out of habit and wanted to kick herself for her politeness.

"Yes?"

"This is Emma Mendell. Are you planning to bail Jason out of jail?"

"I can't," she whispered.

A man's voice boomed in the background. "Who are you talking to?" He didn't give her time to answer, and his voice was closer when he said, "Are you talking to *him*?"

"No!" she said quickly. "It's one of Jason's friends."

Despite the situation, Emma got a little thrill out of being called Jason's friend. Interesting how Alexis had left Emma's name out of it, though.

"Do you know if anyone is going to bail him out?" Emma said quickly. She sensed the conversation didn't have much time left.

She was right. "I can't help you," Alexis said quickly and then there was silence.

Emma looked at her phone to verify that the call was over, and sure enough, the timer had stopped. She looked at Mrs. Patterson.

"That didn't go well."

Emma shook her head. "No, it didn't." She chewed on her lip. "Now what?"

At first Mrs. Patterson didn't say anything. But then she asked, "He's honestly a nice boy? You're not just saying that because you have a crush on him?"

Emma's cheeks got hot. "He's honestly a good person. And I don't have a crush on him."

"Mm-hmm. All right then. I guess we've got to go down to the county jail."

Emma's heart leapt in excitement. "Really?"

"Don't make me say it twice. I might change my mind."

Chapter 29

Emma

Mrs. Patterson had a car! Emma had walked past the woman's garage a thousand times, but she had never thought about what might be in there. If someone had asked her to guess, she wouldn't have guessed a car.

But there was a car. It was ancient and as big as a boat. Emma got the feeling it had been nice in its day, maybe even expensive. Now it just looked clunky and dusty. *Really* dusty.

Mrs. Patterson struggled to bend over so she could grab the handle near the bottom of the garage door.

"Here!" Emma said, moving quickly. "Let me get that for you." At first she thought the door wasn't going to budge, but then it slid upward, making a wicked racket. She flinched, feeling as if Mrs. Patterson had just announced to the whole neighborhood that she was finally stepping out.

Emma hurried back to the boat-car and slid into the front seat, which was surprisingly cushy. With less enthusiasm, Mrs. Patterson slid behind the wheel and turned the key that was dangling from the ignition.

Nothing happened.

Mrs. Patterson said a semi-naughty word that made Emma snicker and feel grown-up. Adults never cussed around her. "I probably should have expected that." She looked at Emma. "Sorry, kiddo. I tried."

Emma's heart raced. "We could take a cab?"

Mrs. Patterson snorted. "A cab? In Carver Harbor?"

"No! There is one! I've seen it. I mean, it doesn't look like a TV cab. It's a banged-up old minivan, but it says taxi on the side, and there's a light on top!"

Mrs. Patterson looked out through the dusty windshield, her hands still on the wheel. "I'm not sure I'm up for a ride in a mysterious minivan taxi."

Emma didn't know what to say. Had they really come this far to fail? She didn't mean to, but she started crying. It was all too much. Her father had lost his mind and embarrassed them all. Her mother was crazy. And now *her* family had caused superstar Jason DeGrave to get thrown into jail. She leaned her head back against the headrest and the tears slid down from the corners of her eyes.

"All right, all right. Don't cry."

Emma wiped at her eyes. "Sorry," she said quickly. She didn't want Mrs. Patterson to think she was trying to manipulate her. She hadn't been.

But it seemed Mrs. Patterson hadn't even heard her. She was climbing out of the car. "I guess you'd better hail us a cab."

"Thank you!" she said more loudly. "I'll call them right now." She quickly searched for the cab company's number, scared Mrs. Patterson would change her mind.

A tired voice answered on the third ring.

Emma was halfway through her second sentence before the embarrassment hit her. She was calling a creepy cab and asking for a ride to the jail?

But the tired voice didn't take on a judgmental tone. She just continued to sound tired. She would be there in twenty minutes.

Fearing that if Mrs. Patterson went back into the house, Emma might not be able to get her back out again, she didn't share the timeline. "They'll be here soon. Let's go wait."

"I heard you ask for the jail, but we've got to go to the credit union first."

"Oh."

"I don't think the jail will take a personal check." Mrs. Patterson slung her ancient purse strap over her shoulder and headed toward the open garage door.

She paused at the threshold.

Emma held her breath.

Mrs. Patterson stepped over the threshold and kept on walking—all the way to the end of her driveway. Then she stopped and turned to watch for the cab.

It had happened. She'd left the house. And the event hadn't been nearly as dramatic as Emma had anticipated.

Mrs. Patterson didn't even look uncomfortable. She just looked impatient. "Are you sure you gave them the correct address?"

"Yes. I know my own address. I just added two to get yours."

She smiled. "Fine, Miss Smarty Pants." She coughed. "When we get in the cab, you do most of the talking."

"Okay," Emma said tentatively.

"And the same thing goes for the jail. I may have been around the block a few times, but I still have no idea how to bail someone out of jail."

Chapter 30

Emma

I t didn't take the cab twenty minutes to arrive. It took them fifty-five.

At the half-hour mark, Emma had sprinted back into the house to fetch a kitchen chair, which she now offered to put back.

"We'll get it later. I don't want this prompt, professional cabbie to drive off without you, and I don't think anyone is going to steal my old kitchen chair."

They climbed into the minivan's middle seat. *Now* Mrs. Patterson looked uncomfortable.

The driver apologized for being late, and Emma reminded her where they needed to go.

"I know. I remember."

"Oh, wait, actually we need to go to the credit union first."

"That will cost you extra."

Obviously.

"What credit union?"

Emma looked at Mrs. Patterson expectantly, but her face was pale and pinched. "Mrs. Patterson?"

"What? Oh. Any credit union will do."

The van started moving, and Emma found tremendous satisfaction in riding by her house, knowing her parents had no idea that she was in a cab on the way to the jail. Her knee bounced up and down nervously, and Mrs. Patterson reached over and put a hand on it. "You're shaking the whole van, and it might fall apart *without* your help."

Emma tried to control her leg.

"Do you want the ATM, drive-through, or lobby?"

This question appeared to perplex Mrs. Patterson for a few seconds. Then, "I need to go inside."

The driver sighed and pulled the van into a handicapped parking spot.

Mrs. Patterson didn't move.

"Do you want me to go in with you?" Emma asked.

"No," she snapped. "I can do it." But she still didn't move.

"The clock's a tickin'," the driver said unhelpfully.

"Come on," Emma said gently, "I'll go with you." She got out of the van and walked around to slide Mrs. Patterson's door open. Then she reached for her hand, but Mrs. Patterson yanked it away.

"I'm fine." She climbed out of the van on her own accord and headed for the door.

A friendly teller welcomed them, and in a soft, timid voice, Mrs. Patterson asked for a withdrawal. She slid her membership card across the shiny counter.

"Thank you." The teller picked it up with impossibly long, shiny, royal blue fingernails. "Do you have a photo ID?"

Mrs. Patterson fiddled with her wallet and produced a driver's license, which the teller studied.

"Um ... this expired a long time ago."

Mrs. Patterson raised her eyebrows. "Well, it's all I've got."

The teller appeared to be stymied.

"I can vouch for her," Emma tried. "I know she's who she says she is."

Apparently, this vouching did not comfort the teller.

"Um ... let me find a manager." She scurried away.

Mrs. Patterson leaned on the counter and put her head down on her arms. "This is taking longer than forever."

"I really appreciate it," Emma said, but she had a feeling that her appreciation didn't mean much to Mrs. Patterson right now.

Several minutes went by, and Emma feared Mrs. Patterson was going to give up and bolt for home, but then a man in a long-sleeved shirt and tie appeared in front of them. He gave them a patronizing smile. "Hello. We require valid photo IDs for shared branching transactions."

As he spoke, Mrs. Patterson slowly inched back from him.

Emma hated it, but she knew they had lost. "Let's go. Maybe we'll have better luck at your credit union."

"No!" Mrs. Patterson pulled her arm away from Emma's grasp. Her eyes were swimming with tears. "I've tried. It didn't work. I want to go home."

They reached the minivan, and Emma forced eye contact. "I know I'm asking a lot of you. But I really need your help. Jason really needs your help. If we go to your credit union, can't we just go through the ATM? Then you won't have to talk to anyone."

Her face grew redder, and she climbed into the minivan.

Emma stood rooted to her spot, and Mrs. Patterson slammed the door shut. Through the driver's open window, she heard Mrs. Patterson say, "Take me home," and Emma ran around the van, not wanting to be left behind.

"Wait," she said, out of breath.

The driver waited.

"Do you have a debit card?"

"Of course I have a debit card."

"Then why can't we use it at the ATM?"

She didn't answer.

Emma couldn't imagine what the problem was. Was she afraid of ATM germs? "I'll do it for you!"

"Fine. Sagadahoc Lincoln Federal Credit Union," she said to the driver.

The driver didn't say anything, but she started driving, and Emma tried to study Mrs. Patterson without getting caught studying her. What was the deal with this woman? She had seemed so normal when she'd been inside her house. Now her face was pale and her eyes red with tears.

They pulled up beside the ATM, and Mrs. Patterson sheepishly handed her debit card over.

"Great. Thanks. What's the PIN?"

Mrs. Patterson gave her the saddest look then, and Emma's heart ached for her. Either she didn't know the PIN or she didn't know what a PIN was.

"Never mind," Emma said to the driver, desperate to prevent further embarrassment for her friend. "We need to go into the lobby after all."

The driver rolled her eyes. "You gals are racking up quite a bill. I don't want to hear any complaints when it comes due."

"I always pay my bills," Mrs. Patterson said weakly.

She was quicker about getting out of the van this time, but when Emma opened the front door for her, she said, "What makes you think they're going to take my ID when the other credit union wouldn't?"

"Just a feeling," Emma said, though she had no such feeling. She just didn't know what else to do.

This teller, who was considerably less smiley and whose fingernails had been chewed down to the nub, didn't even ask for an ID. After two conversationless minutes, Mrs. Patterson had an envelope full of money. Emma was shocked at how much she'd taken out. Surely bail couldn't be *that* much?

Chapter 31

Emma

"This is not the road to the jail," Mrs. Patterson said.

"Pretty sure I know where the jail is," their surly driver said.

"This road goes to the jail," Emma said quietly.

"No, it doesn't." Mrs. Patterson pointed west. "The jail is downtown, right beside the courthouse."

The driver snickered. "Man, you don't get out much. They moved the jail years ago. The old jail is a restaurant now."

"A restaurant?" Mrs. Patterson cried. "Who would want to eat in a jail?"

"Lots of people," the driver said. "If they can afford it. It's a pricey joint."

Mrs. Patterson shook her head and looked out her window.

Emma realized she was holding her breath and forced herself to breathe. She was incredibly nervous about walking into a jail. What was she supposed to say?

Fortunately, it wasn't nearly as creepy as she'd anticipated. The building felt more like an office building than a jail, and the lobby was a wide-open, airy, clean space.

A man behind a counter looked up at her and smiled as she approached. "Can I help you?"

"I need to bail someone out." At that moment, she hated her own voice. She sounded too young. Not confident enough.

The man looked beyond her toward Mrs. Patterson.

"All right." He sat down in front of his computer. "Who would you like to bail out?"

"Jason DeGrave." She tried to sound more confident.

"It's already done," a man's voice said from behind.

Emma whirled around to see Coach Packard had come through a door to her left.

"Hi!" She was astonished. What was her phys ed teacher doing here, and why was he bailing Jason out? Then she remembered that he was also the high school soccer coach. "You've already done it?"

"Yes. Just finished the paperwork, but it's awful nice to see you here trying to help him. I didn't realize you and Jason were close."

Her face grew hot. "We're not ... really." Did Coach Packard not know why Jason had been arrested? Did he not know whose face he had smashed? What were the chances he might never find out? Not very good, she guessed.

Mrs. Patterson took her elbow. "We can go, then."

"Hey," Coach Packard said, looking at Mrs. Patterson thoughtfully. "Are you ... are you *Fiona Patterson*?"

Mrs. Patterson's body went rigid. "We really must be going."

Coach Packard's face lit up. "My goodness! Do you live around here?"

Mrs. Patterson forced a smile. "I keep something of a low profile."

"You don't still play?"

"I do not."

Play what? Emma looked at her friend curiously.

"I am retired," Mrs. Patterson explained.

"I'm sorry to hear that." Coach Packard looked at Emma. "Have you heard her play?"

Bewildered, Emma shook her head.

"Well, you should. If she won't play for you, at least get one of her albums. She is a genius." He stepped closer, still grinning. "She performed for your high school back when *I* was in high school."

It wasn't exactly *her* high school. She was going into the eighth grade. But she didn't mind his lumping her in with the high schoolers. She looked at Mrs. Patterson. She couldn't imagine her performing at anything. And she had *albums*?

Fiona. She hadn't realized Mrs. Patterson had a first name. If she'd ever thought about it, she would have realized that, of course, she did. But she hadn't thought about it.

Mrs. Patterson was pulling her toward the door. "Nice to see you again, but we really must be going."

"By all means." His smile faded, and he looked perplexed. "I'll be sure to tell Jason that you tried to help, Emma. I know that will mean a lot."

Maybe it would. Maybe it wouldn't. She wasn't sure Jason would ever forgive her for being her father's daughter.

"Thank God," Mrs. Patterson said when she saw the waiting taxi. She practically lunged inside.

Emma followed her into the van and then used her phone to search for Fiona Patterson. The processing wheel started spinning. Apparently, the county jail didn't have great cell service.

No one said anything until they were back on the road.

"The coach was right. It *will* mean a lot to him," Mrs. Patterson said quietly.

"Maybe."

"When you get in trouble, not many people come rushing to your aid. And you did, even though you don't know the boy well." She took a deep breath. "You think he's going to blame you for this mess, but he isn't."

How had she known that was a concern? Was she a mind reader?

"You don't blame him for his mother. And he won't blame you for your father."

This was a good point.

The tiny circle on her phone stopped spinning and presented her with a very different image of Mrs. Patterson. She was young. She was posed like a movie star, with big hair and makeup. She was beautiful.

She was also an award-winning classical pianist.

Chapter 32

Esther

Six women filed into the lawyer's conference room. It wasn't a small room, but it wasn't designed for the number of people now in it. Four of them sat down, and Vicky and Cathy hovered behind them.

Attorney Walter Rainwater looked at them curiously. "Are you sure you want all six of you on the deed?"

"Seven," Esther said. "Barbara Silvie wasn't able to make it."

"Gallstones," Vicky explained unnecessarily.

"All right. We'll need someone to get her signature."

The seller came into the room and gave Esther a broad smile. "Glad to see you ladies. Wasn't sure I was ever going to sell that building."

"Why'd you ever have it in the first place?" Vicky asked.

The man shrugged. "My ex-wife wanted to turn it into an antique store, but she never got around to it."

Esther shuddered. That would have been a shame. She was glad God had foiled that plan.

He settled back into his chair. "She never got around to lots of things."

Esther turned her attention to the lawyer. This was the first time she'd seen him. Before today, she'd only spoken to him on the phone. He was quite handsome. She almost laughed at herself for having the thought. She wasn't looking for romance—she wasn't *Dawn*.

He caught her eye and smiled, and her cheeks grew warm. She prayed silently that her cheeks weren't pink.

"So you ladies are starting a church?" Walter sounded bemused.

"Yes," Dawn said. "And you're welcome to join us on Sunday morning at ten-thirty."

Esther gave her a look. To Esther's knowledge, they hadn't decided on a start time yet.

"I might just do that," he said, and he almost sounded sincere.

"Ohh," Dawn said. Was that a coo? Had she just cooed at the man? "Are you a churchgoing man?"

He shrugged. "Not really." He busied himself with paperwork. "I'll need photo IDs for each of you." He looked at Esther. "Does someone have the check?"

Esther nodded toward Cathy. They'd all given their shares to her.

"I do," she chirped.

"All right." He took the check from her outstretched hand. "Then all I need is your signatures." He looked around the room in wonder. "All of them."

Esther's hand trembled as she picked up a pen. This was really happening. She'd put every penny she had into this, but more significantly, she'd put all her *hope* into this. She really needed this to work. She had known she'd needed a church, but now that she had a mission, she thought maybe she needed that too.

A church and a mission. She signed slowly, relishing the moment. It was a brand-new day.

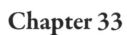

Chapter 33

Emma

Emma's ringtone startled her. No one called her anymore. Not that long ago, her phone had been ringing off the hook with drama from Isabelle and crew, but now it was silent. She wasn't so sure this was a bad thing.

She didn't recognize the number and answered tentatively, hoping it wasn't a political poll.

"Hello? Is this Emma?"

Emma grinned with joy at the sound of her new friend's voice. "Mary Sue!"

"Sorry it took me so long to call. It's really hard to get permission to use the phone around here."

"Permission?"

Mary Sue let out a long breath. "First, my parents said I needed to *give you some space*. Then, we only have one phone in the house, and someone is always on it. But I finally got my turn. I've been wanting to check on you. Are you okay?"

"I don't know." It was true. She didn't know if she was okay. "I think I'm okay? But I'm obviously pretty mad. And pretty embarrassed." It felt oddly good to admit that second part.

"Oh my gosh, don't be embarrassed. It's not your fault. And lots of kids have been through the same thing. I'm sure everyone feels sorry for you."

"I'm not sure I want them feeling sorry for me." She didn't want them feeling anything for her. She didn't want them thinking about her at all.

"I'm sorry. That's not what I meant. I just meant that people are on your side, and no one's blaming you. You're the victim in all this."

"I think my mother is more the victim than I am, but I think I get what you're saying. Thank you."

"What do your friends say about it?"

"What friends?"

"You know. Isabelle and those guys."

Pfft. "I haven't heard from them since this all started."

"None of them?" Mary Sue said after a pause.

"None of them." She understood Mary Sue's surprise. She was a little surprised too. She was surprised that Isabelle hadn't inserted herself into the drama. And she was surprised that Natalie and Raven didn't care anything about her. "Basically, you're my best friend now. Congratulations." She laughed nervously. Maybe she shouldn't have said that. Maybe Mary Sue wouldn't *want* to be her best friend. She'd thought Mary Sue was the weirdo, but that was last week. Now she was the cheating pastor's kid. Now who was the weirdo?

But Mary Sue squealed. "I would be so honored. I'm not even kidding." She giggled. "Is there anything I can do for you?"

"Not that I can think of."

There was an awkward silence, but Emma didn't want the conversation to end, so she tried to think of something to say.

Mary Sue broke the silence. "Are your parents fighting a lot?"

"I have no idea."

"Why, are you hiding out in your room?"

"Not exactly. I'm at my neighbor's house." She smiled at Fiona, but Fiona appeared to have fallen asleep in her chair.

"What neighbor?" Mary Sue's curiosity was piqued.

"Mrs. Patterson. She's wonderful. She's basically letting me live here."

"Live there? Like you've actually moved out of your parents' house?" Mary Sue sounded kind of jealous.

"Not really. Just till all this calms down or until my mom figures out that she needs to leave my father. I don't really know my plan. I obviously want to live with my mom, but not in the same house as my father." Her words felt jumbled as they came out of her mouth, and she wondered if she was making any sense.

"I think I can understand that. You must be pretty angry."

Emma laughed bitterly. "Sometimes. Sometimes I'm just in shock." She sighed. "I didn't see this coming. I knew my father wasn't perfect, but I didn't know he was capable of *this*."

"Is Mrs. Patterson the one who never comes out of her house?"

Emma held her breath, hoping Mrs. Patterson couldn't hear Mary Sue through the phone, but Mrs. Patterson hadn't flinched. She still appeared to be sound asleep. "She doesn't leave very often. She doesn't need to." She felt defensive of her new friend. "She's got an awesome house with a big backyard and a beautiful garden. I don't blame her for not wanting to leave. I don't really want to leave here either."

"Cool. My mom always says she hates leaving home too."

Emma didn't think that was quite the same thing as the Puddys lived on a giant farm. "Yeah." Emma heard voices in the background and a scuffling noise.

"I'm so sorry. I have to go. My dad needs the phone, but let me talk to my parents, and I'll see if I can invite you over again soon. And this time, we won't invite Isabelle."

"Thanks. I'd appreciate that."

"Which part? The visit or the not inviting Isabelle?"

"Both."

"Promise you won't steal my bike and run away this time?"

Emma laughed, and it felt good. She realized it had been a long time since she'd had a genuine laugh. "Maybe. We'll see how it goes."

Chapter 34

Emma

E mma looked around the quiet room. What was there to do now? It was beautiful outside, but she didn't want to venture beyond the safety of Mrs. Patterson's walls. Mrs. Patterson's phobia was contagious, apparently.

She decided she needed to find a book to read. She doubted Mrs. Patterson would have anything good, but it was worth a look.

She slowly stood and tiptoed past the napping woman. There was no sign of books in the living room, but the house was small. If there was a bookcase, she should be able to find it.

Mrs. Patterson's bedroom door was closed, but Emma opened it anyway. She felt a little guilty, but she didn't think she'd get caught. She'd be quick. A scan of the room showed no bookcase. Surely a woman who lived alone and never went anywhere had books somewhere? So where were they?

She backed out into the hallway and looked around. She knew there weren't any books in the bathroom so the only other places to check were the attic and the basement. She had never been in either of those spaces but knew they existed because there were stairs going up and down.

She decided the attic was less creepy and headed up the narrow stairway. As she pushed on the overhead door, she said a silent prayer that she wouldn't be attacked by mice or bats.

Instantly, she wished she'd brought a flashlight. There were no windows up here. A little light came up from the hallway below, but not nearly enough. She couldn't even tell how big the room was. She pulled her phone out of her pocket and turned on her flashlight app—*jackpot*. The space was jam-packed full of boxes. She looked around for any sign of something that might entertain her, and her eyes landed on a clothing rack full of sparkly outfits. She stepped closer and ran her hand down a sequined sleeve. What were these here for? She couldn't picture Mrs. Patterson in any of them. Were these antique prom gowns? When had proms been invented?

Or had Mrs. Patterson worn these when she played the piano at the high school all those years ago? Emma didn't think so.

Turning away from the dresses, she looked around at the boxes, hoping to find something labeled books, but nothing was labeled with anything. She opened the first box to find more clothing—though this batch wasn't nearly as sparkly. The next box held picture frames. She started to close the box again, but her curiosity spoke up. She pulled out a framed photo of a much younger Mrs. Patterson shaking hands with a man in a suit. Emma had no idea who the man was, but his pose suggested he was important. The next picture was of a beautiful Mrs. Patterson at the beach with a handsome man. Was that her husband? Mrs. Patterson never talked about her husband, and Emma had assumed she was a widow, but why had she made that assumption? Maybe Mrs. Patterson had never even been married. She was kind of an odd duck.

She felt guilty for snooping and put the photo back and closed the box, even though there were many more tempting frames. She moved on to the next box. At first she thought this box contained magazines and she got a little hopeful—it might be interesting to read old magazines, see what the advice for women was in the sixties.

Then she realized these weren't magazines. They were records. She snickered. What kind of music had Mrs. Patterson listened to when she was young? Healthy, wholesome stuff? Or the stuff that passed for rebellious back then? She pulled the first album out of the box and gasped. This wasn't an album that Mrs. Patterson had listened to. This was an album that Mrs. Patterson had *created*. She pulled out the second album. It was a different one, but it was still Mrs. Patterson. "Fiona" was splashed across the cover in bold, bright red letters, and "Patterson" was written neatly underneath. A photograph of Mrs. Patterson in the spotlight sitting on the piano bench nearly mesmerized Emma. There was so much more to this woman than she thought. How had she ended up in a small house in Carver Harbor? How had she ended up in a house that didn't even have a piano—

"What are you doing up here?"

Emma whirled around, pulling the albums to her chest protectively. "I'm... s... s... sorry," she stammered. "I was looking for ... books." She flinched, knowing how untrue that sounded.

"Books? I don't have any books!"

Emma pulled the album away from her chest and looked down at the cover. "Mrs. Patterson," she said softly. "These are amazing!"

"No, they're not. Put them away. I don't even know why I still have those. Just haven't got around to getting rid of them."

Emma didn't believe this for a second. Who would throw away their own albums?

Mrs. Patterson pointed at the stairs. "I've invited you into my house, and you have violated my trust. Please, go."

Emma's mouth dropped open. "Go?" Was Mrs. Patterson kicking her out of her house? "You want me to leave?"

"I want you to leave my attic," she said evenly. The anger in her voice suggested that once Emma had left the attic, Mrs. Patterson might want her to leave the rest of the house too.

Emma regretfully put the albums back into their box and then walked past Mrs. Patterson to the stairs. She slowly descended and then turned in case the older woman needed a hand, which she didn't. The trap door slammed shut behind her, and Mrs. Patterson walked past Emma and returned to the living room. "The library has books," she said without turning back.

Emma followed her into the living room and gingerly took her spot on the couch. She still wasn't sure if Mrs. Patterson wanted her to leave the house. "Why don't you want to talk about it? It's all so impressive! You should be proud."

"It's not that I'm not proud. I'm indifferent. None of that means anything to me. It was a different lifetime, and she was a different woman."

Emma didn't understand. "Why did you stop playing? You must have been amazing."

"I was never good enough," Mrs. Patterson snapped. Then, it appeared that she felt guilty. She tipped her head back and closed her eyes. Her voice softened, but it still had an edge to it. "I'm sorry. I'm not trying to be hard on you. I can understand why you might be curious, but I'm telling you, I don't have any good stories to share. There's nothing worthy of your curiosity here. And I'm asking you to please let it go. You're welcome to stay here as long as you need to, but you're not welcome to pry into my personal matters."

She had delivered the words gently, but they still felt like a slap.

For a long while they sat there. Mrs. Patterson stared at the television, and Emma stared at the wall. Emma didn't want to make her angry, but she thought she'd feel better about things if she just talked about them. "You are famous?"

She guffawed. "So famous that you've never heard of me." She sounded bitter.

"That doesn't mean anything. I can't name a single piano player."

She smiled genuinely then and looked at Emma. "I was a little famous, yes, but a lot of good it did me."

"Why? What happened?"

"Nothing happened. Nothing at all."

Emma decided to give up. She wanted to hear about Mrs. Patterson's life, and she thought Mrs. Patterson would feel better if she talked about it, but she didn't know how to force the woman to share. "I guess I'll go to the library." Her library card was at home, and she really didn't want to have to go get it, but she was beyond bored.

"You're coming back, right?" Mrs. Patterson said quickly, worriedly.

"Of course. Do you need anything while I'm out?"

She shook her head sadly. "Be careful."

Emma snickered uncomfortably. What could go wrong between there and the library? She left the house and walked across the adjacent lawns and then stopped in her driveway. Both her parents were home. She didn't want to deal. Maybe the library would lend her books without the card. She would tell them that she lost it. Deciding this was the way to go, she turned away from her house and headed in the opposite direction, toward the library.

As she walked, she did another internet search for Fiona Patterson. She'd seen the pictures, but maybe there was some music online. This time, she read the bio more carefully. Mrs. Patterson had won a lot of awards and played with a lot of people in a lot of places. Emma didn't fully understand most of what she was reading, but she could tell that it was impressive. She followed a link to some online samples. Mrs. Patterson's records were still for sale. They were even available on CD. It occurred to Emma that this was how Mrs. Patterson lived, how she paid the bills. She must still be getting money for her music. Emma pressed play, and the sound that came out of her small phone speaker made her stop walking. It sounded like three different people playing three different pianos. Was that what she was listening to? No way that was only one woman's hands. She stopped and pressed a different sample button. This song was faster and sounded even more complicated. She stared down at her phone. Mrs. Patterson could play the piano like this? This was amazing! She didn't know anything about classical music, but she'd been listening to piano music every Sunday for her entire life, and she'd never heard anything like this.

Chapter 35

Emma

The librarian watched her nervously and then hurriedly said, "Of course" when Emma explained that she couldn't find her library card.

Did this woman know who she was? Did she know what was going on in her life? She was acting so uncomfortably that Emma thought she knew everything. Or was Emma being paranoid?

She left the library as fast as she could and kept her head down as she hurried back to Mrs. Patterson's.

"Emma!" a voice called out from behind.

She turned to see Jason with two of his friends. They each eyed her curiously, as if they were looking at a bug under a microscope.

"Hey, Jason," she said self-consciously. She wished he hadn't seen her.

He started closer, and her breath caught. She fought the urge to back away. She was grateful that his friends stayed behind.

"Hey, I just wanted to thank you. Coach Packard told me what you tried to do. I would've called to thank you, but I don't know your number."

He paused, and she wondered if he was waiting for her to give him her number. She decided that was preposterous and bit her lip.

"Anyway, it was super nice and thoughtful of you. I was shocked, actually. And I'm really sorry I beat up your dad."

She raised an eyebrow. "You are?"

He smiled and shrugged. "Well, yeah. I'm probably going to have a record now." He laughed. "But really, I *am* sorry. I'm not your dad's biggest fan, but I shouldn't have done what I did. I was just so angry, and I wanted to do something about the whole thing, even though there really wasn't anything I could do."

She nodded. "I understand. I've felt that way too."

He grinned again. "All right then." He playfully punched her shoulder. "You take it easy, Emma." Then he turned and headed back to his friends, who were still staring at her.

She rushed home, now glad she had ventured out to the library, no matter how weird and awkward the librarian had been.

She found Mrs. Patterson back in her chair drinking what looked like iced coffee. It looked yummy. The ice clinked in her glass as Mrs. Patterson eyeballed her over its rim. She swallowed and let out a satisfied sigh. "Did you find anything good?"

"Don't know yet, but I got some possibilities. And I ran into Jason DeGrave."

"At the library?" Mrs. Patterson cried, as if that were the most preposterous thing she'd ever heard.

"No." Emma snickered. "I saw him on my way home. Anyway, he was really nice, and he thanked us for trying to bail him out. He also apologized for beating up my father."

Mrs. Patterson raised her eyebrows. "Is that right?" She clicked her tongue and turned back to the television. "Just when you think people can't surprise you anymore."

Was she talking to Emma? Or herself?

"Is there any more iced coffee?"

Mrs. Patterson's face fell. "Oh. Sorry. I'm afraid this isn't iced coffee. It's coffee brandy. I often have a little nip in the afternoon and evening. I haven't been since you've been around. Don't want to be a bad example and all. But I thought"—she paused— "I thought you would take longer at the library."

Emma smiled. "Sorry. I hurried. I felt like I was being watched."

"You probably were being watched."

This didn't help her feel any better. She opened one of the books and started to read. It wasn't bad. There was a little too much romance, but other than that, it seemed it was going to be a solid end-of-the-world story.

She was vaguely aware that Mrs. Patterson got up and went back to the kitchen. Then she returned and flipped through the television channels. Emma stretched out on the couch and tried to focus on the words in front of her.

But when Mrs. Patterson made her third trip to the kitchen, Emma got curious. She sat up and listened. Ice clinked against glass, and then Mrs. Patterson was back with another serving of creamy brown beverage.

"That stuff must be pretty good."

"Tastes terrible, actually. Don't ever try it."

Emma had never been around anyone drinking alcohol before, and it made her feel grown-up. She tried not to stare, tried to act as if she was used to people swigging coffee brandy all the time.

"I didn't like it the first several dozen times I tried it." Mrs. Patterson laughed at herself. "But after a while, I developed a taste for it." She took another swallow. "I'm grateful I don't have more of a problem. I don't drink much, just enough to take the edge off."

The edge off what, Emma didn't know. "Why did you keep trying it if you didn't like it?"

Mrs. Patterson let out a long sigh. "I was young and trying to fit in. I didn't know yet that I would never fit in. *Could* never fit in."

"Fit in with who?" As soon as she had asked, Emma knew. The music people. "The other musicians?"

She nodded slowly. "The other musicians. The managers. The agents. The producers. The supporters." She gave her a sardonic look. "You know the rock stars have fans coming out of the woodwork, but that's not how it was for us classical folks. We had to beg for fans."

"But you're still selling albums."

Mrs. Patterson looked at her sharply.

"I saw them online."

"Just because they're for sale doesn't mean someone's buying them."

"Oh."

She took another drink, and her ice tinkled again. "I sell a few here and there. I guess I should be grateful. It helps pay the bills. But I'm not exactly swimming in the dough."

There was a long pause, and Emma tried to think of a way to keep the conversation going. "Is that why you stopped playing, because it wasn't making much money?"

"No. I never cared about the money. I just wanted to make good music, but I was never good enough. I quit because I got tired." She leveled a gaze at Emma. "You probably know that artists are the sensitive type."

Emma thought about it. Had she known that? She wasn't sure. She thought about the kids who hung out in the art room in school. The emo kids. The goth kids. Yes, they were the sensitive type, weren't they? She nodded enthusiastically.

"Well, I was the most sensitive of the sensitive. It made me a good musician, but it also made me a bad musician."

Emma frowned. She didn't understand.

"It's not that I couldn't take constructive criticism. I could, when it was constructive. But Emma..." She stopped talking and stared at the television.

It felt as though she was about to share something big. "What?"

Mrs. Patterson shook her head. "I shouldn't be giving advice. I'm not qualified."

"I wasn't asking for advice. I'm just interested in who you are."

She smiled, looking thoughtful. "Who I am and who I was are two different people. Who I was was a fragile flower, and everybody who stabbed me in the back, who stole from me, manipulated me, who insulted me, betrayed me... all those people. It was just more than I could take. There was no one good in the world except for my husband." Her voice got thick. "And then he left too."

"Is that when you..." She didn't know how to politely phrase her question.

Mrs. Patterson did it for her. "Is that when I started staying in my house?" She chuckled. "No. I think he left me because I started staying in the house. He married the girl who got up on stage and flounced around and smiled for the cameras. When I decided I couldn't do that anymore, he grew tired and he left, the last betrayer in a long line of betrayers."

Emma's heart cracked for her. She sounded so lonely. "I'm so sorry. Does he live around here?"

"No, he died years ago. Got in a bad car accident with his new wife. She was twenty years younger than me, and that irritated the snot out of me, but I still didn't wish them pain or death." She finished her glass and set it on the end table beside her. "I don't think I should have any more brandy. It's given me the gift of gab. So you got your story after all. Please keep it between us. I don't think anyone around here knows my past, and I'd like to keep it that way. I don't really like attention, and it's not a very good story anyway. I think they'd end up disappointed."

"I won't tell anyone."

She nodded gravely. "If you can keep that promise, it'll be the first promise anyone has ever kept for me."

Emma had never felt greater resolve to keep a secret. She would prove it to Mrs. Patterson, prove that people weren't all bad, that they weren't all cruel. "Don't you miss playing?"

"Oh, of course I do," she said quickly. "But when I play, all I can hear are my mistakes." She looked at her curiously. "Do you play any instruments?"

Emma shook her head. "My mom took piano lessons for years, but she was always terrible. She would get so frustrated that she would cry and bang on the low keys. Learning an instrument never looked like much fun to me."

Mrs. Patterson laughed appreciatively. "Sounds like your mother and I have more in common than I might've once thought."

"How old were you when you learned?"

"I was five when I started. I was a natural. If I had kept playing naturally, I might've been okay. But I tried to get trained. That's when everything started going wrong."

"Trained? You mean like lessons?"

She nodded. "Lessons upon lessons. Then Juilliard."

"Juilliard? Isn't that that fancy music school in New York City that no one can get into?"

Mrs. Patterson laughed. "Indeed it is. I am an alumna."

"Wow. I'm impressed."

"Don't be. I'm also a woman who doesn't leave her house."

"You left your house when Jason needed you."

She shook her head. "That was different. That was an emergency."

Emma waited for her to make eye contact and then gave her a sly smile. "Well then, I guess I have to find you more emergencies."

Chapter 36

Esther

The thunder clapped so loudly that Esther jumped. She looked at the ceiling. "I sure do hope the roof holds."

Cathy looked up. "I do too, now that we own it."

"Don't you have any more money tucked away for a new roof?"

"Vicky!" Esther scolded. Thus far, no one had discussed the size of Cathy's donation, and Esther thought that was best. They'd been shocked by it, because Cathy was such a tightwad, but once Esther had thought about it, her surprise had faded. Cathy had worked at a great job. Her frugalness had probably allowed her to grow a healthy nest egg.

"Sorry," Cathy said. "I have no more money. For real this time."

Vicky chuckled humorlessly. "The roof will hold. There was no water damage in here. If it hasn't leaked the last thirty years, it probably isn't going to leak tonight."

Esther thought that might just be her luck. Since they were about to fling open the doors tomorrow morning, the roof might just give in. "I hope you're right, Vicky. But that sounds like a horrible storm. If it doesn't pass, I might be sleeping right here."

Rachel put the last screw into the wobbly altar railing. She was the handiest one among them. She was the only handy one among them. "There." She winced as she came to her feet.

Vicky looked around the sanctuary. "I'm not sure why we're all freaking out, acting like tomorrow is opening night. I doubt anyone is going to come."

"They'll come," Rachel said confidently.

"How do you know that?" Vicky demanded.

"First of all, curiosity is a strong motivator. People want to know what we're doing in here, so they'll come check us out."

Esther thought she was dead wrong about that. Curiosity might be strong when there was a new restaurant in town or a car wreck nearby, but she didn't think the principle applied to churches.

"Second," Rachel continued. "I blasted the invitation all over social media."

"You did?" Vicky cried. "What were you thinking?"

Cathy laughed. "Why is that a bad thing, Vicky? Just because you don't know how to use social media doesn't mean someone else can't."

"It's not that I don't know how to use it," Vicky hissed. "I just prefer not to. It's all foolishness. But my point is, you can't go blasting it all over the internet. Who knows who will show up?"

"Vicky," Esther said, "we *want* people to come. *All* the people. If Rachel wrote something on social media and what she wrote brings in a weirdo, well then that weirdo needs Jesus, and we will be glad he is here."

Vicky looked disgusted. "We don't want weirdos. Weirdos drive off the good families."

While Vicky's point made some practical sense, Esther still thought her theology was dangerous. "We'll welcome the good families and the weirdos."

Vicky rolled her eyes.

Dawn was staring across the room with her hands on her hips. "While you're spending all this time on the computer, Rachel, have you sold the organ yet? We owe Barbara's son for lumber."

"Lumber? What for?" Vicky said. "He hasn't done anything yet."

Barbara glared at her. "He hasn't done anything because he hasn't had the lumber. He also works sixty hours a week."

They all stared at Rachel expectantly. "About that." It was evident that Rachel did not want to share whatever it was she had to share.

Esther had a pretty good idea of what Rachel was holding back. Esther had done some of her own research and knew that the original plan of selling the organ for a sudden influx of cash was not going to be as easy as she'd thought.

"Well," Vicky said. "Spit it out."

Rachel took a deep breath. "Nobody panic, but from what I can tell, we won't be able to sell this organ."

"What?" Vicky cried. "What does that mean?"

Rachel scowled at her. "It means just what I said. We can't sell it."

"That doesn't make any sense," Vicky said. "If you said we can't sell it for *much*, then I can see the cause for alarm, but you said we can't sell it at all. Of course we can sell it."

Rachel shook her head slowly. "If we were to sell it, we would have to pay someone to come take it apart and move it. And that process costs more than the organ is worth. We might, and I stress might, be able to give it away, but I don't even know if we could pull that off. I saw several other churches trying to give organs away, and there weren't very many takers."

"Give it away?" Vicky cried. "We're not going to give it away!" She glared at the organ as if it had personally offended her. "And it can't just sit there. It's enormous!"

"I think it can sit there just fine," Esther said. "It's not hurting anyone, and it's not like we're desperate for space."

"But it's enormous!" Vicky said again.

"If it's going to sit there, we ought to use it," Dawn said.

"About that," Rachel said. They looked at her expectantly again.

Barbara sneezed and cried out in pain. Three of them said "God bless you" in unison.

Rachel asked, "Gallstones?"

Barbara nodded sadly. "Sneezing with gallstones hurts more than having a baby."

Esther snickered.

"Never mind that," Vicky said with a distinct lack of sympathy. "What about playing the organ? Does it work?"

Rachel nodded. "It works. I fiddled with it a little. But it badly needs to be cleaned, and it needs to be tuned."

Vicky looked disgusted. "It's not like any of us can play it."

"We'll put that on our to-do list," Esther said, eager to put the matter to rest. "Once we get the plumbing fixed and the ramp built, we can hire someone to clean and tune the organ."

"That would be a gigantic waste of money," Vicky said.

"Well, we don't have to argue about it until the money exists," Esther said. She was glad there were seven of them so there would never be a tie vote. She dreaded the day that one of them went to heaven.

The thunder crashed again so close that Esther felt it in her bones. The lights flickered, and then everything went black.

Chapter 37

Tonya

Roy sat hunched over his laptop screen. Tonya had asked him twice what he wanted for dinner, and both times he hadn't responded. She didn't know if he was ignoring her or if he was so engrossed in whatever was on that screen that he didn't hear her.

The elders had given him two months to seek the Lord and find his way back, but Tonya had not seen him open a Bible in the week since.

It occurred to her that she hadn't opened her Bible either, but she shook the thought out of her head. She wasn't the adulterer in the scenario.

"Pretty fierce thunderstorms out there. You might want to unplug the computer. "

The mouse kept clicking.

She carried her bowl of cereal into the living room to watch television, even though she'd seen every show ten times. She missed Emma so much that her chest hurt. She texted her, "You're not out in this, are you?"

Emma answered quickly. "I don't go anywhere, Mom. I'm tucked in safely with Mrs. Patterson. You should come over."

Part of Tonya desperately wanted to do just that. But another part of her knew she was supposed to stay by her husband's side. It was her job as a wife, and it was the only way she could see to fix this mess.

The landline rang. Tonya ignored it. It never rang for her. If someone wanted her, and no one did lately, they used her cell phone. The landline meant someone in the church was in need.

On the fourth ring, Roy loudly said, "Will you please get that?" His words were civil; his tone was not.

She hurried to answer the phone before the answering machine picked up. When she heard Elder Frazier's voice on the other end of the line, her stomach fell. Something was wrong. "Everything okay?"

"I don't mean to be short, Tonya," he said gently, "but I really need to speak to Roy."

She carried the cordless over to the desk and held it out toward her husband. Her arm was trembling.

"What's wrong?"

She didn't know. She didn't even know how she knew something was wrong. But something was. The air around her felt thick and heavy.

"Hello?"

She strained to hear Elder Frazier but she couldn't hear anything. She watched the blood drain out of her husband's face, and she knew. They were firing him. How? They'd told him that he could keep his job. How could they change their minds like this? How could they yank the rug out from underneath her? And just like that, she knew that someone had complained. Someone was unhappy with the elders' decision.

Roy murmured some polite words and then hung up the phone. He dropped it on the desk and fell back against his chair. It wheeled away from the desk, and he sat, a droopy shell of himself.

She didn't dare to ask. She had to know. "Well?"

"Well, what?"

"What did he say?" She hated him for making her ask.

He turned his head toward her, and his eyes looked like snake eyes. "Get out."

What? What had he said? She stood there stupidly.

"Get out!" he said more clearly and with more volume.

Because she didn't know what else to do, she laughed. "Get out where?"

"I don't care. Just get out. I can't stand the sight of you."

She thought she was going to throw up. Her shaky feet took her to her guest bedroom. She shut and locked the door behind her and then sat on the edge of the bed. Why had he told her to get out? How was that the logical next step from whatever the elder had said?

He pounded on the door so hard that it shook. "Get out! I said get out!" He was coming unhinged. He was out of control, and she was directly in the path of his madness.

She stared at the closed door. "And where exactly am I supposed to go?"

"I don't care where you go." He talked to her as if she were a stupid, filthy dog. A nuisance. "I only care that you do go. We've been thrown out of the parsonage." He said this as though it were her fault. "So pack your bags and go."

"Please, Roy, calm down."

She'd said it with love, but it only enraged him further. He pounded on the door so hard that she feared his fist would come through it. "I am your husband and I am telling you to get out of this house!"

"Where am I supposed to go?"

"I don't care. As long as you're not here."

Chapter 38

Tonya

The tears came so fast and hard her eyes felt like they were on fire. Someone had thrown dynamite at her flimsy dam, and now the water gushed out. Her throat grew so tight that she had to fight for air.

"Please, Roy. Don't do this." She hated the weakness in her voice. She didn't think he'd even heard her.

"Go with your daughter. You've managed to turn her against me, so you two might as well be homeless together."

Anger kindled some strength. "Turned her against you?" Was he serious? "Roy, I haven't done anything. I didn't have an affair! This is all on you."

"If you don't move out of this house, I will move you out!"

She almost laughed. He wasn't a burly man. She knew he couldn't sling her over his shoulder and carry her outside.

"I'll start with your things. The things you care most about. I'll go get the photo albums." She heard him walk away.

She didn't know if he would really throw Emma's baby photos out into the storm, but she didn't want to chance it. She opened the bedroom door and stuck her head out into the empty hallway. She stepped out tentatively, afraid he was going to pop out from behind something and grab her. But he didn't. She found him on his way to the front door with an armload of scrapbooks and photo albums. "Roy, please, no." She reached for the albums, but he yanked them away from her.

"If you get out now, I'll give you a few days to gather your stuff. But I'm serious." His voice was like a growl. "I really can't be in the same house as you right now." He shifted the books to one arm and then reached out and opened the door. The wind blew rain in at them. She didn't know where her raincoat was. She didn't know where an umbrella was. She looked out into the storm. He pulled the books back, threatening to heave them out into the rain.

"Fine. I'll go." The evenness in her voice surprised her and pleased her a little. She couldn't believe she hadn't already crumbled into nothing. Anger was a powerful glue. "Sixteen years I've given you," she said softly. "Sixteen years of my life. My entire adulthood I've given you." They'd gotten married in Bible college. She'd never been an adult without him. Had no idea how to be an adult without him. "I've given everything of myself to your church, to your career. I gave you a daughter, and she's the best human being in the world. And you're going to throw us both away?"

His face twisted up into a knot she'd never seen before. She did not know this man. Had she ever known him? She thought so. But the man she knew was missing—if not gone altogether. She stepped out into the rain, and it stole her breath. He tried to slam the door behind her, but it hit her hip and bounced open again. She was knocked out onto the top step, and he kicked the door shut. This time, it stayed shut.

She looked toward Mrs. Patterson's house. Her outdoor light was on, like a small lighthouse. Thunder crashed, and Tonya jumped. Mrs. Patterson's lighthouse light flickered and then went out, as did all the streetlights. The town plunged into a howling darkness. She hugged her arms around her chest and started across her lawn. Would Mrs. Patterson even open the door? It would be okay if she didn't, Tonya decided. If Mrs. Patterson wouldn't let her in, she would get Emma to come out, and they would find somewhere to go together. She had a whole church of people who were eager to serve, eager to help others. As long as she and Emma were together, she could survive this, she told herself. A sob erupted out of her. She started across Mrs. Patterson's yard. The rain was so loud, it almost mocked her own crying, making her problems seem small and insignificant.

Could she survive this? And if so, how? How would she endure this humiliation? How would she put a roof over Emma's head? How would she feed her? How would she buy her school clothes? She raised her hand, hesitated, and then knocked on Mrs. Patterson's door.

Chapter 39

Fiona

"Did you hear that?" Fiona looked at the door. The hair on the back of her neck stood up, and her heart rate increased. Was she being paranoid, or had someone just knocked?

She heard nothing but the wind and almost laughed at herself. No one would be out in this storm.

"No," Emma said without looking up from her phone, "I didn't hear anything."

Mrs. Patterson lit another candle, and the noise came again. "I think there's someone there."

Emma got to her knees on the sofa and pulled the curtain back from the window. She gasped. "It's my mom!" She flew to the door.

Fiona's chest tightened. Emma's mother had come to get her. Emma was leaving her. That was all right, she told herself. The child did not belong to her, and Emma would be better off with her mother. Still, her absence was going to hurt.

Emma flung open the door and jumped out into the rain to wrap her arms around her mother. Over the wind, Fiona could hear them both crying.

The door started to swing shut, but Fiona grabbed it and opened it wider. "Get on in here, out of the rain." She stepped back to make room, and they came inside, arms still wrapped around each other like they were a single entity. Fiona shut the door. How different her life might've been if she'd had children. Maybe she wouldn't be so alone.

Emma stepped back to look at her mother but she didn't let go of her. "What happened?"

"Your father threw me out."

"*He* threw *you* out?" Fiona cried. That didn't make any sense. Was there more to the story than she'd heard?

The pastor's wife took a long shaky breath and tried to wipe her chin with her wet shoulder.

"Hang on. Let me get you some towels." Fiona hurried to the bathroom. When she returned, the two were speaking quietly.

Tonya looked at her and explained, "The church just fired him. And his first reaction to that was to kick me out. I guess he was only keeping me around to keep his job."

Fiona handed her a towel, unsure of what to say.

"You can stay here!" Emma said, her face bright with youthful hope. She looked at Fiona. "Isn't that right?"

Fiona nodded. "Of course. There's not much room, but if you don't mind being cramped."

"She can have the couch. I'll sleep in a chair."

"I don't want to put you out," Tonya said. "I'd be grateful for a roof for the night. Then, tomorrow, we'll find somewhere to go."

"I don't want to go anywhere," Emma said. "Mrs. Patterson has been awesome through all this. I can't just abandon her now."

Tonya closed her eyes. "Let's discuss it tomorrow. I'm a little overwhelmed right now."

This admission spurred Fiona into action. "Of course you are." She pulled the kitchen chair away from the table. "Here, please have a seat. You want me to get you some dry clothes? We're about the same size."

Tonya shook her head and sat down. "No, thank you. I'm drying out already."

"All right. Let me at least get you some hot tea, take the chill off."

Tonya nodded. "That would be nice."

Hurriedly, Fiona grabbed the teakettle, filled it with tap water, and then stopped. "I'm sorry. I wasn't thinking. I don't have a way to get the water hot."

"That's all right. That's sort of how my whole month has been going. You think of something reasonable, rational, something normal, and then something irrational kicks you in the face and you wonder how you ever thought anything could be normal."

Fiona stopped moving, and the teakettle slowly lowered to her side. She stood there staring at Tonya. She could identify so strongly with what Tonya had just said. She'd been kicked in the teeth so many times by things completely unexpected, by people she'd thought would never hurt her. "Well then, let's go to the living room. It's more comfortable there."

She led the way into the even smaller room.

"Your home is lovely," Tonya said, and Fiona got the impression she would have said that no matter what her home looked like.

"Thank you. It had better be because this is where I spend my time."

Tonya smiled through her tears. "I'm sorry we've never met before." Her expression reminded Fiona of a politician.

Fiona studied her. "Do me a favor."

"Sure."

"Drop the niceties. You are a woman in crisis. Act like it."

Tonya's head snapped back a little, and then she studied Fiona in return. "I'm sorry. I'm not quite sure how to act, I guess. I've never done this before."

Fiona smiled, trying to look comforting. "No need to be sorry."

"I was just trying to be polite."

"I'm sure you were. But there's no need." Fiona laughed. "I'm not asking you to be *im*polite, of course, but Emma and I decided a while ago that we would dispense with pretense."

Tonya looked at her daughter curiously.

Emma shrugged. "Mrs. Patterson isn't into acting."

Tonya returned her gaze to Fiona. "I guess I can appreciate that."

"I used to be a performer," Fiona said, surprised at how easily the admission came this time. "I got enough of that for a lifetime. Forcing a smile when you felt like throwing up. Thanking them for coming when you wished they hadn't."

Tonya snickered, and her body physically relaxed.

This slouching brought Fiona significant joy.

"Why would you not want them to come?" Tonya asked.

"Because by then I knew what they really thought of me. They were pretending to want to be there, and I was pretending to want them there. It was a ridiculous make-believe existence. The only real things in my life were the things I fought to keep hidden and buried."

Tonya's mouth fell open a little. She didn't say anything for several seconds, and then she said, "You wouldn't believe how much I know what you mean."

Chapter 40

Tonya

Emma had promised her the couch, but it wasn't working out that way. Her daughter had tipped over and fallen asleep with her head in her lap, and Tonya was relishing the opportunity to run her hand over her daughter's soft hair. How she had missed that hair.

It was late, but Tonya didn't know how late. The storm had passed, but the power was still off. Knowing this section of Maine, she didn't expect it would come back on soon. Their town was stuck out on a peninsula, so they were usually one of the last to get power restored. She didn't mind. She found the candlelight comforting. She found Fiona's presence even more comforting. The woman wasn't at all what she'd expected.

"You know, I've tried to learn to play the piano."

Fiona tipped her head sideways like a curious puppy. "Emma mentioned something about that."

Tonya laughed dryly. "You can't even imagine how bad I was at it. I don't understand how anyone can read three or four or even more notes at a time and make their fingers do all those different things at the same time." She'd started out trying to pay Fiona a compliment, but now thinking about her life as a pastor's wife was making her feel sick to her stomach.

"Did you take lessons?"

She nodded. "I sure did. More than a year of them."

Fiona scowled. "Usually, a teacher will only have you read and play one note at a time so that you're not overwhelmed. Then, when you can play one note, you move on to two. Then, when you can play two, you move on to three. I don't think you had a very good teacher."

She shrugged. "She was all right. She tried. I don't think I was a very good student."

"Why was that?"

She didn't like the intensity with which Fiona was studying her. "I guess I didn't really want to be doing it at all. I mean, I wanted to be a good pastor's wife, and all good pastors' wives should play the piano, right?" She forced a laugh. "But there was all this pressure, and I—"

"Pressure from who?"

"I don't know. My husband. The piano player who wanted to retire. And myself, maybe."

She nodded thoughtfully. "I found that pressure and art don't mix well together. Often, the appliance of pressure makes art not art anymore." She grabbed a new candle from the end table beside her, got up, and went to the coffee table at Tonya's knees. She lit the new candle with the nub of the other and then pried the spent candle out of the holder with knobby fingers.

Tonya tried to imagine those fingers dancing across the ivories. "I wish I could hear you play sometime."

Fiona didn't say anything. She just carried the old candle back to her chair and then set it on the end table.

"Is that why you stopped playing? Did the pressure make the art not art anymore?"

Fiona shook her head. "That happened, but that's not why I stopped. I stopped because I didn't want to be around people anymore. It hurt too much."

When she didn't elaborate, Tonya said, "I'm sorry."

"I know you are."

"So you don't see anyone, ever?"

She shook her head, avoiding eye contact. "Don't need to. Don't want to. Much safer right here with the imaginary characters on television."

Tonya looked at the black screen. "I've noticed myself that sometimes I enjoy those fictional characters more than the people in my real life. It's not fair. All those people have a room full of writers making them likable."

She'd been kidding, but Fiona didn't laugh. "It never bothered me much if someone was unlikable. I figured that was their prerogative. What I couldn't tolerate was the cruelty."

"Cruelty?"

Fiona put both hands on her armrests. "You know what? I could use a glass of coffee brandy. I know you're a pastor's wife and all, but would you like a glass?"

Her lips started to object before she even realized how tempting the offer was. How odd. She'd never been tempted by alcohol before. "I've never had coffee brandy."

She stood. "Do you like coffee?"

"Very much."

"Then you'll probably like coffee brandy. I'll get you some. If you don't drink it, I will."

Chapter 41

Tonya

Tonya stared at the drink on the coffee table. Most of her had no intention of touching it. But there was one small voice telling her that she should. And that voice was growing louder with each passing second. *Oh, who cares? It will make you feel better. Fiona's drinking it, and she's not a bad person. She's not drunk. It's just one drink. It will help you relax. Haven't you earned a few minutes of relaxation? And just* think *of how horrified Roy would be if he found out you had a drink with Fiona!*

"Do you want me to take it now?" Fiona's glass was still mostly full, but apparently, she could see the struggle.

Tonya shook her head quickly. "I'm fine."

Fiona chuckled. "I know you are. I just don't want to lead you into the darkness."

Suddenly, she was desperate to show Fiona that her beverage choice was not *darkness*. She quickly reached out and took the wet glass. "No, no, you're not." She looked around the dark room, trying to find something else to talk about. She ran her free hand through her daughter's hair. "Thanks for letting Emma stay here. She really didn't want to be anywhere near her dad."

"I don't think he kept you around to keep his job."

She looked up. "What?"

"You said the only reason Roy was keeping you around was to keep his job. I don't think that's true. I think that, now that everything's falling apart, he's going to grasp at the only thing that gives him pleasure, and that's the other woman."

Tonya tried to process that. "Doesn't that amount to the same thing?"

Fiona shrugged. "Maybe. Maybe not. One is more insulting than the other, I think."

Tonya didn't know which theory was the more insulting, but she wasn't sure she wanted to figure it out. "Either way, my pastor husband just kicked me out of my house."

"The house that he is also being kicked out of. He is feeling powerless, and so he wanted to make someone else feel powerless. Now he's going to go to the other woman and let her lick his wounds."

Tonya noticed that this idea didn't make her jealous. Disgusted, yes, but not jealous. "Maybe." Without thinking, she took a drink. Then she looked down at her hand in surprise. Had she forgotten what was in the glass? She winced, but then Fiona chuckled, so Tonya tried to hide the wince—too late. "It tastes a little like fire." But the creamy aftertaste was lovely. She tipped her head back and closed her eyes, waiting to feel whatever it was that alcohol made one feel.

She felt nothing.

"It's the champagne of Maine!" Fiona said in a ridiculous voice, and Tonya looked up to see her lifting her glass into the air and wearing an equally ridiculous expression.

"Is it? I didn't know." She took another tentative sip, and then looked at Fiona. "Is it really, or did you just make that up?" Either way, it was pretty funny. If she'd made it up, Tonya was impressed.

Emma stirred, and a tremor of guilt traveled through Tonya. She put the glass back on the coffee table.

"I don't think it's the champagne of anything, but that was a joke back in the sixties. I used to drink *actual* champagne back then because I had things that I thought were worth celebrating, but my mother loved the coffee brandy when it first came out." Her expression sobered. "She was not a problem drinker, nothing like that. She was a great mother in every sense. But she was also a sensitive soul, and I think a drink in the evening helped ease the hurts of the day."

Tonya was desperate to discuss something more uplifting. "What were you celebrating?"

"What?" Fiona had gotten lost in a memory.

"What were you celebrating with the champagne?"

"Oh, that." She shrugged. "Awards. Albums. Weddings. My wedding." She gave Tonya a crooked smile. "I can commiserate with what you're feeling right now, but I can also tell you that being a divorced woman isn't so bad."

Tonya wasn't sure she should believe that, coming from a woman who was scared to go outside. The drink beckoned to Tonya again, and she picked it up and took a long drink before she could talk herself out of it. She told herself to stop feeling guilty. It wasn't a sin to drink a single drink. Some Christians drank all the time. Not *her* family, of course, but some Christians. She started to feel warmer and more relaxed. She let out a long breath and tipped her head back again to enjoy it.

"You're going to be all right," Fiona said softly. "I know you don't believe me, and that's all right. But months or years from now, when you're happy and at peace, remember that I predicted the future." She laughed and took another drink.

And Tonya followed suit.

"You know, I'm not the only ex-performer in the room," Fiona said.

Tonya looked at her, not understanding.

"You've been something of a performer too these last several years. And I'm thinking that you're going to appreciate being able to retire from that gig."

What was she talking about? She wasn't a performer. Was she talking about the failed piano playing? "I never actually played in public—"

Fiona blew out a puff of air. "I'm not talking about the piano. I'm talking about being a pastor's wife. All the smiling." She waved her hand around. "All the greetings. All the weddings, the showers, the graduations, always having to show up and act excited." She shook her head. "It must have given your mouth cramps, all that smiling."

Tonya chuckled. "Yeah, actually. I never thought about it that way, but I did have to fake some of that joy."

"Joy *and* peace. I'm sure things weren't perfect in your life. And yet you acted like they were. You listened to other women's problems and acted like you didn't have any." She said it all without an ounce of criticism.

"Yeah. Maybe." She had never thought of it as acting. She'd just thought of it as looking put together. If she was going to help people, she had to be put together. No one in a mess wants to be helped by someone else in a mess.

"Maybe schmaybe. Well, congratulations. You don't have to perform anymore. For anyone, ever."

Tonya wasn't sure this was good news. If she wasn't a pastor's wife, then who was she?

Chapter 42

Esther

There was a crazy excitement in the air. Even Vicky was acting chipper.

At ten minutes past ten, a giant family walked through the doors, and Esther's eyes filled with tears. She wiped them away quickly, not wanting their first visitors to think she was daft, and went to greet them.

"Welcome, welcome!" she said, extending her hand to the wife first. She was out of her comfort zone, but she couldn't possibly have felt more welcome in her heart. "I'm Esther."

"Lauren Puddy," the mother said. "This is my husband, Roderick."

The man took her hand and pumped it up and down. "Pleased to meet you." The man's smile was warm and genuine.

Esther looked down at the kids, whose clothes were worn and faded, but everything fit and everyone was clean and healthy-looking.

Lauren pointed to each of the children. "Victor, Mary Sue, Judith, Carolyn, and Peter."

"What great names!" Esther said and meant it. "My mother was a Carolyn."

Lauren smiled broadly. "Thank you. Yes, they are all named after family."

Esther stepped aside and swept her arm across the sanctuary. "Well, welcome. Make yourself at home." She pointed toward the only bathroom. "The restroom is over there." She pointed toward a table in the back. "And help yourself to coffee and doughnuts."

At the word *doughnut*, all the kids looked, and the littlest piped up, "Can we, Mom? Can we?"

"Maybe after the service." She started to herd her children down the aisle. She gave Esther a broad smile as she passed. "Thank you."

Esther was still watching them settle in when Barbara tapped her on the arm. "Who's going to ring the bell?"

Esther frowned. "I don't think anybody is."

Barbara stepped back in horror. "Of course someone is! We discussed this, remember?"

Esther did remember, and she was pretty sure that they had decided that they didn't know if the bell could even ring, they didn't know how to test it, and they didn't know if trying would get one of them killed.

Cathy tried to come to Esther's rescue. "We did discuss it. We decided it wasn't safe."

"*We* didn't decide anything!" Vicky said. She was never one to pass up an argument. "And I wasn't even there *to* decide!"

Oh, that's right. They hadn't had a quorum for the great bell vote.

"Vicky," Esther said. "Have you been up there? It's pretty treacherous."

"I *have* been up there. And it's a piece of cake. There's a rope hanging from above. You pull the rope, the bell swings, and we get church bells! How is that dangerous?"

Realizing the new family was within earshot, Esther tried to remain patient. "That is one old rope. It could be rotten. And we don't know if the bell will even swing. It could be rusted in place. Or it could swing, then break off, and go crashing down through the floor."

Vicky rolled her eyes. "If it's that rusted and loose, then we shouldn't even be in here under it."

She had a point. Esther hadn't thought about that. She looked up to make sure she wasn't standing directly in the line of fire.

The Puddy father stood and turned toward them. "Would you like me to take a look at it?"

No one answered him. They were all too shocked.

"He's quite handy," Lauren said without looking up from the child she was attending to.

Roderick smiled and climbed over his children's knees to reach the aisle. He looked at Esther. "Just lead the way, ma'am."

Esther led him to the back of the sanctuary and up the narrow stairway that led to the steeple. She tried to go fast and tried not to pant, so by the time she got to the top, she feared she was going to have a heart attack. She looked at the giant bell. "I'm scared to touch it." Speaking revealed how winded she was.

Roderick whistled and ran his hand along the bell. "She sure is a beauty." He walked around the bell. "Yep, I found the rope. I can see why you're hesitant. I think a good yank would pull this thing apart."

Esther gave Vicky a satisfied look.

"I've got a stepladder in my truck," he said, and Esther quickly looked over the railing toward the street. That giant family had come in a *truck*? But there were two vehicles she didn't recognize. Either someone else had shown up, or the Puddys had come in separate vehicles.

Suddenly, he was standing right in front of her. "I'm pretty sure I've got some rope too. Let me see what I can figure out. I'll inspect the wood on the headstock, and if it's good, which I think it might be, I'll replace the rope."

Esther was stunned. Who was this angel? "All right."

He smiled and looked past her. "If you'll excuse me."

Oh, of course. She was blocking the top of the stairs. "Sorry." She stepped away, bumping into Vicky as she did so.

"Ow!" Vicky cried.

"Well, you knew I was coming. You could've gotten out of the way."

Chuckling, Roderick headed down the stairs.

Chapter 43

Emma

Emma startled and looked out the window. Church bells? Where were those coming from? She went closer to the pane and peered outside. "Do you guys hear that?"

No one answered her. She looked around but couldn't see either woman. She stepped outside for a better listen. She'd lived in the neighborhood her entire life and she'd never heard church bells. Of course, she was always *in* church at this time, so maybe her church's walls were just too thick. Or maybe there were too many kids making too much noise.

She didn't think either of these theories was true. She thought these church bells were new, which made her even more curious. She stepped off Mrs. Patterson's steps and followed the sound. They were coming from at least one block over, but she didn't want to go all the way around the block, so she crossed the street and stopped at the edge of the neighbor's lawn. Then curiosity nudged her across the lawn and into their backyard. She looked around to make sure she was alone, and then she slipped through the hedge and into the adjacent backyard—which, it turned out, did not belong to a house. It belonged to a church. An ancient one.

This building had always been here, she realized. But it wasn't a church, was it? It looked abandoned, and she'd never seen anyone there. There was someone there now, though, because the bells had just rung, and there were cars parked along the street.

Sad that the bells had stopped, she followed the edge of the building toward the front. What an ugly building! The paint was peeling, and some of the windows were boarded up. Those that weren't boarded up appeared to be brand-new and were surrounded by unpainted plywood.

She reached the front to find an older woman standing on the front step. "Good morning!" the woman cried cheerily, waving enthusiastically.

Instinctively, Emma jumped back.

"Oops! Didn't mean to scare you off."

The church kid inside her scolded her for being rude. She stepped back into the woman's sight. "You didn't scare me. Just startled me is all." *Lame.*

The woman looked ridiculous. She wore a huge red hat that was at least five times the size of her head, and a necklace of chunky green beads that perfectly matched her bright green dress. She looked like a giant red tulip.

The woman was still smiling. "Would you like to join us?"

"No, thank you! Have a great service!" Emma ran back the way she'd come.

Chapter 44

Fiona

Church bells? What on earth? Fiona looked out her bedroom window. It sounded like they were coming from the old, abandoned church on the next block over. But who would be ringing that bell and why? Had they started that church back up again? If so, *great*. Just what this town needed—more churches. She rolled her eyes.

Then she noticed her young friend Emma tiptoeing across the street. She stopped at the edge of her neighbor's lawn and then continued right across it. Fiona shook her head. Hadn't Emma ever heard what curiosity did to the cat?

Fiona watched her disappear, and her chest tightened. She forced herself to breathe. Emma would be fine. She wasn't a little kid. Just because she'd gone out of sight didn't mean anything bad was going to happen to her. She was going to have to get used to Emma going out of sight. She and her mother wouldn't be with her much longer.

Chapter 45

Tonya

C hurch bells? Tonya looked out the bathroom window but couldn't see anything. She went into the kitchen and looked out a bigger window. But what was she looking for? She knew there was no church within sight.

Except that there was. The old abandoned church on Providence Ave. She stepped outside and looked up. She could clearly see the old steeple peeking above the neighboring roofs. It certainly sounded like the bells were coming from there, but why? Had someone started that church up again? She looked at her phone. It was ten-forty. Who starts a service at ten-forty? Had some kids broken in and started ringing the bell? She almost laughed at the foolishness of that theory. Kids did get up to mischief, but not usually on Sunday mornings.

She looked around for Emma and saw her slipping through the hedge across the street. She thought about following her, but she knew she looked a fright, and she feared there was liquor on her breath, so she slipped back inside.

Fiona was back in the kitchen. "What do you make of that?"

Tonya shrugged. "No idea."

"You churches don't talk to each other?"

"That's the thing! We *do*. I know what's happening at every church within twenty miles, but I have no idea what's happening over there. That place has been empty for years. It's not even owned by a church anymore. Someone bought it privately."

"Who would want that place?"

Tonya shrugged. "I can't imagine." A small panic fluttered through her. Would a new church pilfer the people from her church? Then she was reminded that her church wasn't her church anymore.

"I take it you're taking this Sunday off?" Fiona said gently.

Tonya nodded. "I can't go."

"Sure you can, if you wanted to. You can do anything you want."

Tonya sighed. "No, if I went, it would be like saying that I support their decision to terminate my husband."

"Well, don't you?"

What? Of course she didn't. Wait. Maybe she did. A little. "I don't know. But I can't walk in there. I can't face those people, knowing what they know. I could barely stand it last week, but I had to do it to help us keep our jobs, to help us keep our home. Now there's nothing to fight for."

Fiona was studying her.

"What?"

"You said *our*. *Our* jobs. Were you employed there as well?"

"No, but I might as well have been. It was a full-time job."

"Without pay."

Tonya held her arms out to her sides. "My rewards are eternal."

Fiona looked skeptical.

Emma came rushing back inside. "Did you guys hear that?"

They both nodded.

"There's some weird lady standing on the front steps inviting people inside."

Tonya laughed. "Weird lady? What does that mean?"

"Okay, well, she's not *weird* exactly. She was just ... I don't know. What she was doing was weird, that's all. And there were about ten cars there."

"Ten? Really?" So maybe they were starting a new church. Though who "they" were was a complete mystery.

"Whose cars?"

Emma gave her an incredulous look. "I don't know! I don't know what everyone in Carver Harbor drives! Besides, I didn't even look at the cars, just noticed that they were there. You want me to go back and look? Take down some plate numbers?"

Tonya looked at her quickly. She didn't know if she was joking.

"I'm kidding. But not about going. Wanna go check it out?"

Tonya was beyond surprised at the question. "Do you?"

Emma shrugged, looking sheepish. "Let's go see what it's all about. If it's creepy, we don't have to stay. And remember, we've got to find a new church."

"Not today we don't."

Emma looked disappointed.

"I'm sorry, honey. I just woke up. I don't have a change of clothes or my makeup ..." She didn't add the concern about liquor breath. "I can't go anywhere right now, let alone a new church." The idea of presenting herself to a whole new batch of people made her stomach cramp.

"They'll probably be there again next week," Fiona said, breaking the silence.

Tonya looked at her new friend. "I promise I will get a plan together soon, but I am really, really tired. Do you mind if I lie down for a little while?"

Fiona gestured toward the couch. "Make yourself at home."

Emma followed her into the living room and then looked down at her. "Are you hungover?"

She forced a laugh. "I only had two drinks."

Emma folded her arms across her chest, waiting for a more definitive answer.

"No. I promise, I am not hung over. I'm just tired." She rolled over. She was more tired than she'd ever been. Her eyes burned, her throat hurt, and she just couldn't face her to-do list yet. She couldn't think about facing anything. She just wanted to close her eyes and not think.

Chapter 46

Esther

Esther sat in the back pew and admired the backs of the congregants' heads.

Roderick Puddy was a man they needed to keep around. Not only did he have a lovely wife and five awesome children—he knew how to fix things. They'd thanked him profusely, and it had been revealed that they'd learned about New Beginnings from one of Rachel's social media posts. Apparently, Lauren was some distant cousin of Rachel's.

Amazing.

Across the aisle from the Puddys sat their lawyer, Walter Rainwater. And he was still handsome.

All seven founding ladies were in attendance, and all seemed pleased as punch—especially Vicky who was somehow making announcements last for fifteen minutes. Esther cleared her throat and glared at her. Vicky avoided her eyes but did wrap things up.

Then Rachel stepped forward to lead the music. "We don't have a musician yet, but one is coming," she said confidently. "For now, would you please find 'How Great Thou Art' in your hymnals? I'm sorry, I can't give you a page number, because we've got a mishmash of hymnals, but I checked, and they all have 'How Great Thou Art.'"

The page rustling faded out, and Rachel, looking very nervous beneath her giant red hat, began to sing the old song in a strong, unflashy alto. Others soon joined in and drowned her out, and she looked relieved. Esther sang as loudly as she could. She'd never seen Rachel look nervous before. So they were *all* out of their comfort zones. Except maybe Vicky. "God," Esther prayed as she sang, "send Vicky a little something. Get her out there on the edge with the rest of us."

They sang two more songs, and it seemed no one missed the piano. Then Cathy stepped up behind the ancient pulpit. She cleared her throat. She too looked nervous. "First things first. I am *not* a pastor! I am not a biblical scholar. I am not a preacher. I am not even a teacher. And I am not going to pretend to be any of those things. I've never worked anywhere but the paper mill, and I raised three awesome children. But neither of those things qualifies me to stand up before you here today.

"I am here now because I am a God-fearing woman who has spent years in the Word. God is sending us a piano player, and he's sending us a pastor. Until then, we'll have laypeople up here sharing what God has put on their hearts. Today, God has put on my heart a vision for this church, and I'm going to share it with you.

"First, let's read what Jesus had to say in the twenty-fifth chapter of Matthew." She put on her reading glasses with a shaking hand. Then she read, "Then shall the King say unto them on his right hand, 'Come, ye blessed of my Father, inherit the kingdom prepared for you from the foundation of the world.'" Without raising her head, she looked out over the top of her glasses and gave everyone a delighted, almost mischievous smile. "Doesn't that sound delightful?" It took her several seconds to find her place again, but everyone waited quietly and patiently. "So then Jesus said, 'For I was hungry, and ye gave me to eat. I was thirsty, and ye gave me to drink. I was a stranger, and ye took me in. Naked, and ye clothed me. I was sick, and ye visited me. I was in prison, and ye came unto me.' Then shall the righteous answer him, saying, 'Lord, when saw we thee hungry, and fed thee? Or athirst, and gave thee drink? And when saw we thee a stranger, and took thee in? Or naked, and clothed thee? And when saw we sick, or in prison, and came unto thee?'" She paused, and when she continued, her voice was thick with emotion. "And the King shall answer and say unto them, 'Verily I say unto you, inasmuch as ye did it unto one of these my brethren, even these least, ye did it unto me.'"

Cathy took off her glasses and gazed out at her small audience. "This church is being started by seven old broads."

A few of the women tee-heed.

"We all came from the same church, which shut down. I have no criticisms of that church. I really don't. We had good lives there. Most of us raised our families there. But when I was presented with this opportunity, I had a thought. What if this is our chance to do something better? Something more than just *church*." She put air quotes around the word church. "Nobody is expecting anything of us here. We don't have any expectations to live up to. We can just do whatever God wants us to do, and I think he wants us to feed people, to give people water, to take people in, to give people clothes, to help sick people, and to visit people in prison." She let that sink in for a moment and then added, "I'm not volunteering for the prison run, but I think it's a great idea for someone else."

Everyone laughed. Even the kids. Even Vicky.

"I don't know what it's going to look like yet, but we've got this building and we've got the Gospel. So I say we start collecting food and clothing and bringing it in. We start inviting people. You

know"—she leaned on the pulpit—"I've read that there is some
debate over the interpretation of the Scripture we just read. Does
the least of these mean the least of everyone or the least of the
believers? I don't speak or read the original Greek, so I have no
idea, but I do know that it doesn't matter. God's not going to get
angry at us if we give food to someone who will never be his child.
And if we give whatever we have to whoever is in need, we're bound
to cover all the people he *does* want us to cover. And I'm not going
to dismiss anyone as not being his child, because even if they're
not, they might be tomorrow or the next day, and it might be
our water that brings them to Jesus! Who knows? Stranger things
have happened!" She was getting herself increasingly wound up.
"I taught Sunday school for two decades, and I'm happy to teach
Sunday school again. But let's not *only* glue cotton balls on paper
lambs. Let's also teach our children to get out and minister to
people, to *help* people! Wouldn't that be wonderful?"

At first no one answered her, and Esther wondered if the
question had been rhetorical.

Then Roderick Puddy shot one fist into the air and yelled,
"Amen!"

Chapter 47

Tonya

Tonya pulled her small load out of Fiona's ancient dryer. Emma had sneaked into the parsonage on Sunday night to gather some supplies, but they still had precious little. Tonya knew she had to go pack up her things. Even if the separation wasn't permanent, she was still moving out of the parsonage.

And eventually, they had to move out of Fiona's too. Tonya was in no hurry for that. The woman had been a saint. But it was a small house, and they were living on top of each other.

Still, the hours had ticked by, turning into days. Now it was Tuesday afternoon and they were still there. She had to do something. She had to make a plan. But she was overwhelmed by a million different emotions, and they were paralyzing her.

These emotions took turns sitting in the front seat, but the most frequent occupier was simply embarrassment. How could she leave this house? How could she step foot in this town? She had been the pastor's wife—always respectable, and now she was the woman who couldn't keep a man. She was the woman who couldn't keep a *pastor* from going astray! What a horrible wife she must have been, they would all say.

And right on the heels of this embarrassment came regret and shame. *Had* she been a bad wife? She hadn't been the warmest, the most forgiving, the most nurturing. She'd often chosen to stay in her own lane and do what needed to be done, without worrying about Roy's needs, about Roy's feelings. Had she been affectionate enough? Attentive enough? Apparently not.

And then came the anger. Yes, she had been. She'd done the best she could, and even though she hadn't been perfect, she had always *tried*. And she certainly hadn't stepped out and committed adultery. With a woman from *their church*. She couldn't believe he had cheated, and she was furious, but the part that made her most furious was that he'd done it with a woman from their church. And second to that was that he'd done it while Emma was still a kid. This all would be so much easier if he could've waited until she had moved out on her own. Of course, who knew? He could have been doing it for *years*. Maybe he was doing it before they even had Emma. How would Tonya have known? She was the gullible fool who still wouldn't know if Isabelle hadn't spilled the beans.

Poor Emma, having to hear about it from the likes of Isabelle. This made Tonya think of Isabelle's mother, and she wanted to be sick. She fervently hoped she never had to see that woman again.

But she was thankful that Isabelle's mother wasn't the only woman in the church. There were others, good women, women who would help her get back on her feet.

So why hadn't they called? Why hadn't the head of women's ministry called? Why hadn't any pastor's wife from any other church called? Was she a pariah? Was she contagious? Did they fear they would catch it from her and then their husbands would run out and find mistresses?

She hated her life. She wanted to skip town, start over somewhere new, but Emma had a life there. She loved her teachers, and they loved her. She loved her friends. She was a standout student, a shoo-in for student council, the catcher on the softball team. Could Tonya rip her away from all that?

She went into the living room and collapsed on the couch. She suddenly understood perfectly well why Fiona never left the house. She looked around the room. But that wasn't exactly true because Fiona did leave the house.

Tonya went into the backyard and found Fiona throwing handfuls of leaves and sticks over her fence. She snickered. "Do the neighbors mind?"

Fiona briefly looked up. "If they do, they're keeping their complaints to themselves. The big stuff I put out front for when they pick up spring cleanup. I'm just tidying up a bit from the storm."

"I've never seen you put anything out front."

"That's because I don't aim to be seen. I take out my trash and recycling every week, but I do it long before the sun comes up." She stood up and stretched her lower back. "I'm like a sneaky ninja."

Tonya laughed. "Where did Emma go?"

"She went back to the library. She'll be back soon. You doing all right?"

"No." Her phone buzzed in her back pocket. She whipped it out so fast she almost dropped it. She didn't recognize the number. "Hello?" she said tentatively.

"Tonya? This is Lauren Puddy."

"Oh!" Breath rushed out of her. So there was someone who cared whether she was dead or alive. "How are you?"

"I'm good. Listen, I'm sorry I haven't called sooner. My wise husband has been insisting that I give you some space. We didn't want to seem like we were trying to get the gossip, but I started to worry that you would think I didn't care, and that's just not true. So how are you?"

Tonya collapsed into an outside chair and filled her in, while Fiona puttered around her, pulling weeds and pinching the tips off herbs. "Sorry," she said after a tirade, "didn't mean to unload on you."

"No, no apologies necessary. I think you're right that one of your first steps is to find a new church. We will help you all we can, but you need an army of good soldiers to surround you with their shields. You know, we found a delightful little church right near our old one."

"You did?" They had? They had left the church?

"We did. We saw something about a new church on Facebook, and we went without expectation, just to check it out. We figured we'd spend weeks, if not months, church shopping, but—"

"You do know that they fired Roy, right?"

Lauren hesitated. "Yes."

"So you don't need to leave the church."

Another hesitation. "Honestly, Tonya. We'd been a bit restless there for a while. And the truth is, the elders *didn't* fire him at first. It was only after someone made a stink. If they'd stuck with their decision to stand by him, we might have tried to stay. But it's all this shiftiness. It's all bending and swaying and trying to keep everyone happy. I don't mean to be critical. I'm sorry. We just didn't feel comfortable there anymore. And my kids have been picked on mercilessly, which makes the whole leaving *much* easier."

"I'm so sorry. I didn't know that was happening to your kids." She thought about it. Had she known? Had there been signs?

"Don't be sorry! Because we are really excited about the new church. I would love it if you would be our guest this Sunday, unless you feel God calling you somewhere else. This church has been started by some senior ladies who really want to focus on serving within the local community. Roderick is all fired up about it. And there aren't very many people yet, and certainly no kids except for ours, but I have a feeling that will change. And Emma would have Mary Sue, at least."

Tonya didn't want to go to a weird little church one block away. "I'll think about it. Thanks for the invitation."

"You're welcome. In the meantime, why don't you and Emma come over for dinner tomorrow night?"

"I don't think so. I'm sorry." She was reluctant to commit to anything, especially socializing.

"No worries. I understand."

"Thank you, Lauren. I might not be the most receptive person right now, but I sincerely appreciate you reaching out." She said goodbye, hung up the phone, and looked up at Fiona.

"The longer you stay away from people, the easier it is to stay away." Fiona winked at her. "Not even a warning. Only a fact."

Chapter 48

Tonya

Tonya sat alone in the backyard, trying to enjoy the late summer sunlight.

Her phone rang again. She looked at her screen. This time the caller was in her phone book. It was Missy, Elder Frazier's wife. "Hello?" she said with an excitement that embarrassed her a little. She did have a few friends!

"Hi, Tonya. I'm so sorry to be the one to tell you this, but we really need you to remove your belongings from the parsonage."

It was a blow to the stomach, and Tonya doubled over. No "Are you okay" or "I'm so sorry about what you're going through" or "Is there anything we can do?" Only: "Get out of our way."

"Are you there?" Missy asked.

"Yes," Tonya managed.

"I hate to rush you, but we've got an interim pastor coming in with an entire family."

Tonya had no words for how much she didn't care about the interim pastor.

"So can you do it?"

Tonya couldn't breathe. She didn't know what to say, and even if she could find the words, she wasn't sure her lungs could find the air. She dropped the phone into the grass. This felt good. If she'd hung up on Missy, Missy could have said she'd been acting like a brat, but leaving the phone line open and staying silent? That was more obnoxious, and therefore, more satisfying. She got up and went inside.

Emma had just come into the kitchen with an armload of books. After one look at her mother, her face went pale. "What's wrong? What happened?"

Tonya shook her head and forced herself to inhale. It hurt her lungs. "Nothing happened. But the church just called, and we need to get our stuff out of the parsonage."

"You're kidding." Fiona stepped into the room.

"I am not."

"When?" Emma asked.

"She didn't say. I think that means right now."

"Right now?" Emma cried. "They only fired Dad like two days ago! What if they change their minds?"

Tonya studied her daughter. Was Emma harboring that hope? "Honey, I don't think they're going to change their minds."

"Why not? They've done it once already!"

Tonya's mouth was bone-dry. "I know, but it's a lot easier to fire someone than to unfire them. I'm sorry, honey. That was a final decision."

"Don't be sorry to me! I don't care if he's a pastor or not. I don't think he deserves to be a pastor! I just think they're a bunch of wusses, and I don't like them pushing you around!" She turned and stomped out of the small kitchen.

Should she scold her for disrespecting her elders? Maybe. But she didn't have the energy. She looked at Fiona. "Do you mind if I put some stuff in your garage?"

"Of course not. But I don't think all your possessions are going to fit in the garage."

That brought tears. But they weren't tears of sadness. They were tears of frustration and self-pity. What was she supposed to do? How could anyone do a good job in this situation? "I wonder how much it costs to rent a dumpster."

"A lot, I would imagine. But it doesn't cost anything to drop stuff off at Goodwill."

Tonya nodded. She'd never been much of a Goodwill patron. She never had much stuff to give away. "I can do that. But what am I supposed to do with the furniture? I can't move all that by myself."

Emma came back into the room. "I'll help. We'll get as much as we can as fast as we can, and if there's stuff we can't lift, we can call Mary Sue's dad."

"I'm not going to call ..." She stopped herself. She shouldn't rule anything out. She needed to swallow her pride and get this done. How could anyone be successful given her circumstances? This was how. She needed to call the Puddys. "Hang on. I'll call." She went back outside, fished her phone out of the grass, and then went back inside and looked at her daughter. "Our phones will probably get shut off any second. They're on your father's account."

Emma shrugged. "My only friend doesn't have a cell phone."

At first Tonya didn't know who she meant, but then she realized she meant Mary Sue.

"Hey, Tonya!" Lauren sounded too chipper.

"Hey, remember how you said you were willing to help?"

"Of course."

"Well, boy do I need your help."

Chapter 49

Emma

Neither car was in their driveway, or what used to be their driveway.

"Mom, where's your car?"

"I don't know. He probably sold it."

"Already?"

"I don't know," she said again, sounding irritated.

Emma pulled her phone out and, for the first time since she'd found out about the affair, texted her father. "Where is Mom's car?"

The door was locked, but her mom quickly located their hide-a-key rock and let them inside. Emma stepped through the door, and at the familiar smell of the place, homesickness washed over her. Her eyes burned with tears, but she tried to hold them back. She wanted to be strong for her mother. This was probably even harder on her.

Most of the stuff in the house was already gone.

Her mom whistled. "Wow, your dad's been busy."

"Don't call him that."

Her mom gave her a sad look and then pulled her in for a hug. She kissed her on the top of the head. "I'm so sorry that this is all happening to you, Emma, but he is still your dad. I know that he loves you. He just doesn't love *me*." She let her go.

Emma lost her battle with the tears. "If he loved me, he would never have done any of this." Her phone chimed, and she pulled it out of her pocket.

"It wasn't her car. And it's gone."

"Gone? Gone where?" she texted back.

"Who is that?"

Emma shoved the phone back into her pocket. "No one." She looked around the almost empty room. "Well, at least he's done most of the work for us."

"I wish I had some boxes."

They heard someone pull into the driveway, and Emma went to the window. "It's the Puddys." She giggled. "Looks like all of them. And they brought two vehicles."

Her mother came to stand beside her. "Can they even fit into one vehicle?"

"I think so?"

Mrs. Puddy knocked on the door, which was still ajar. "Yoo-hoo!" she called.

"Come on in," Emma's mom called back.

She stepped inside, and her family followed her in.

"Thanks for coming," her mom said. "We were just wondering, can you all fit into your van?"

Mrs. Puddy laughed. "Sort of. Our seats can be collapsed into the floor, and well, one of them is stuck like that. We'll fix it eventually, but we also thought maybe we could use the truck. Where are we moving your stuff to?"

Her mother looked at the floor. "I'm taking some of it next door, but most of it's going to Goodwill."

At first no one said anything, and her mother looked up.

"Why Goodwill?" Mrs. Puddy asked.

Mr. Puddy slid a hand onto his wife's shoulder. "Don't try to revise the plan, Lauren."

Her mom looked around the room. "What do I need any of this for? A thousand books for women's Bible studies? I will never be allowed to lead one of those again. A million dishes for entertaining? A gazillion pie plates and cake pans?" She looked at Lauren. "And don't get me started on all the church dresses. I plan to never wear pantyhose again."

Mrs. Puddy nodded. "Okay, I hear you. And Goodwill is a good plan. But just for conversation's sake"—her husband groaned—"our new church is stocking an almost empty kitchen. We could take any cookware and dishes you don't want. And we're starting a clothing closet."

"Oh ... I think I like that idea better. Keep it local, keep it free. What a great idea. Then we don't have to drive it all the way to Belfast." She sighed. "I hadn't even thought about how much gas that would take, and I have no money." She put her hands in her back pockets. "And my car seems to be missing."

"Dad sold it."

Her head snapped around. "What? How do you know that?"

"I texted him and asked him. He said it's gone."

Fresh tears sprang to her mother's eyes, and Mrs. Puddy wrapped an arm around her shoulders. "One thing at a time. Let's get you moved. Then we'll find you a car."

Her mom wiped her tears away with the back of her hand and sniffed. "Thank you."

"Sorry, Mom. Where do you want me to start?"

She tipped her head back and closed her eyes. "Would you and Mary Sue take some trash bags upstairs? My suitcase is in my closet. Fill it with my unmentionables—except for the pantyhose. You can throw those away—and the clothes I wear around the house. Keep the jeans, T-shirts, and anything else you know I like. Then put all the other clothes into the trash bags."

"Sure, Mom." She looked at Mary Sue and then started toward the kitchen cupboard that held the trash bags.

"You can give away all the bedding too. Put that in the trash bags." She looked at Lauren. "We've had a lot of house guests over the years. We have enough bedding to run a hotel."

Chapter 50

Tonya

Tonya, Emma, and the Puddys sorted, stacked, packed, pitched, moved, and cleaned for four hours. Roderick and his two sons took all the furniture that was left and moved it to their new church's front lawn, where they put up a "Free to those in need" sign. Roderick had respectfully asked about each of the first several items, but finally, she'd told him that she didn't want a single stick of furniture. Nor did she want any of the lamps. She couldn't believe how many lamps they'd accumulated over the years.

She was in full-on purge mode. If and when she and Emma found somewhere else to live, they would start with new stuff, even if the new stuff wasn't new. She'd rather have someone else's freebies than look at the furniture that reminded her of her old life.

Next, they took all the art she'd had hanging around the house. None of it was worth any money. She'd only bought the things to fill the empty walls.

Roy had taken everything that belonged to him, even his dresser of the matching set, which made it even easier for her to donate her dresser to the church. He'd taken the two televisions, the computer, and their collection of old glass bottles.

Emma and Mary Sue came down the stairs dragging trash bags. "Thank you, honey."

"You're welcome." Emma grunted. "Are we putting these in the Puddys' truck?"

"Yes, please."

"What about the appliances?" Roderick asked, out of breath from his last endeavor.

"Those were all here when we got here, as was the piano."

"Oh good."

She almost laughed at his relief.

Lauren came back inside with an armload of empty boxes. "Your entire kitchen has been moved to the church. If you change your mind about any of it, let me know, and I can smuggle something back out for you."

"Where did you get the boxes?" Tonya asked.

"Grocery store. I brought them back in as I thought we could tackle your books next."

Tonya looked at her bookcase. "Oh boy."

Lauren nodded. "Oh yes." She stepped closer. "I have never seen this many cookbooks in my life."

"Yeah, I don't think the church is going to want these. Maybe we should go to Goodwill after all."

"Actually, I think we should start a library at the church. So I'll take anything remotely Christian over there. But the bookstore on Seven Street buys used books. You might be able to get some cash for the others." She looked at her. "Or even for all of them. You don't have to donate any books to the church."

Tonya let out a long breath. This was all too much. "I'm pretty sure every book other than the cookbooks would fit into a church library, so take it all. We can throw the cookbooks away for all I care."

"No, no!" Lauren said quickly. "If you're going to throw them away, just give them to me! I've been making the same meatloaf for nearly twenty years."

"Do *not* mess with my meatloaf!" Roderick called from another room.

The girls came back inside. "What do you want us to do next?" Emma asked.

"What's left upstairs?"

"Just my bedroom and your jewelry box. And there were some boxes of stuff I didn't go through." Emma scrunched up her face. "Looked personal."

"You girls go tackle Emma's room. I'll take care of the rest."

The girls headed away.

"And Emma?"

She turned back.

Tonya couldn't believe what a good sport she was being. "I know I'm not keeping much, but that doesn't mean you can't. You can pack up every ounce of your bedroom and take it with you."

Emma nodded and gave her a small smile. "Thanks, Mom."

Tonya watched them go and then looked toward the stairs. She couldn't avoid it any longer. She needed to go finish Roy's bedroom.

With so much gone from it, the room looked huge. The imprint from the bed left an embarrassingly clean rectangle on the otherwise dingy carpet.

Her jewelry armoire stood staring at her, challenging her to deal with it. Would she need any jewelry in her new life? She flipped open the top lid. Yes, she still needed the string bracelet Emma had made for her in Vacation Bible School. And she still needed her grandmother's class ring, for sure. She sifted through earrings and costume necklaces. She didn't want or need any of those. Those were purchased to snazz up old dresses and to support the multitudinous women in her church who had tried to make a living selling Grace Space jewelry. She put the few keepsakes in her pocket and moved into the closet where those "personal" boxes were kept.

She pulled them from the shelf and sank to the floor. One of them was the shoebox for the satin sandals she'd worn for her wedding. She lifted the cover to find some of Emma's school photos. They were out of order, and some were missing, but they were all beautiful. Under them lay some of Emma's art, stretching all the way back to a preschool finger painting.

Tonya smiled broadly as she pulled a clay blob out of the box. Second-grade pottery class. Emma had explained that it was a dish for her wedding rings. A sob exploded out of her, and her head fell forward. It was suddenly too heavy for her neck, and she tipped over sideways, curled into the fetal position, and let herself sob.

This was too much.

She couldn't do this.

It was going to kill her.

Why was this happening to her?

Why, God? How could you let this happen to me?

She didn't hear Emma come in, but suddenly she felt an arm slide over her waist. "It's okay, Mom. I got you."

Chapter 51

Tonya

"There's someone at the door," Fiona said in a panicky voice. Tonya pulled back the curtain to peek out the window. Who would be knocking on Fiona's door this early on a Wednesday morning? Or this early on any morning for that matter? She couldn't get a good look at the man in front of the door from her angle, but he was wearing a brown uniform. UPS delivery man, maybe? She had a feeling that it wasn't someone so benign as a UPS driver.

"I'll get it." As she neared the door, her dread grew. She tried to shake it off. She was getting to be as bad as Fiona, fearing the front door.

"Don't answer it!"

He knocked again. "Sheriff's Department! Open up please."

"I don't think we have a choice." Shaking, she reached for the doorknob.

A serious-looking young man in a deputy uniform stood in front of her. "Good morning, ma'am. Are you Tonya Mendell?"

What could this be? Was someone hurt? Or worse? She forced herself to nod.

He handed her a large brown envelope. "You've been served." He waited for her to take the envelope from his hand and then he turned and walked away.

She stood there in shock holding the stupid envelope. Served with what? Was she being sued? That didn't make any sense. She'd never done anything sue-worthy in her whole life.

"What is it, Mom?"

Emma's voice spurred her into action, and she stepped back and closed the door. She didn't want to open the envelope. She had to open the envelope. With trembling fingers that felt thick and uncooperative, she unfolded the metal clasp and then lifted the sticky flap. She slid the papers out. Big black letters on the top right glared out at her: Complaint for Divorce.

Emma looked over her shoulder and gasped. "Oh, Mom."

"It's okay," she said to comfort Emma, even though she didn't know if it was okay. She didn't know if any of this would ever be okay.

"Divorce papers?" Fiona asked from behind.

Tonya nodded without looking at her.

"That didn't take him long."

Fiona had a point. Why was he in such a blasted hurry? Did he have somewhere to go, something to get to, someone else to be? How could he be so good at something he'd never done before? Had he been mentally rehearsing his moves for months? For years? She set the papers on Fiona's kitchen table and looked at Emma. "These don't mean much to me. I don't plan to respond. He can play his games, but I'm not going to let it affect me."

For a moment, no one said anything, but then Fiona said to Emma, "Would you give me a second with your mom?"

Emma looked to her as if for permission, and she nodded. Emma slipped out of the room. Tonya looked at Fiona expectantly.

"Unfortunately, you don't really have the option of doing nothing." She pulled out one of her kitchen chairs and sat down.

Tonya sat across from her. "Why not? I thought doing nothing was always an option."

Fiona raised her eyebrows. "Well, maybe it's an option, but it's a terrible one."

"I'm sorry, Fiona. I don't want to get caught up in all this drama. Let him do his thing. I'm not agreeing to anything."

"You guys have money saved for Emma's college?"

The nosiness of the question surprised Tonya. She nodded. "How did you know?"

Fiona shrugged and studied her hands. "You seem like that type of mother. And you have other savings?"

"Not really. We have a savings account, but we are constantly dipping into it for emergencies."

Fiona nodded understandingly. "If you do nothing, he will get everything."

"He can't take Emma's college savings."

"Yes, he can. And I'm betting that he will. He also might try to take Emma."

"He has shown no interest in Emma so far," Tonya said quickly.

"I could be wrong. I tend to assume the worst about people, but I'm wondering if he might try to get Emma just to hurt you."

Tonya's first reaction was that this was ridiculous. But then she wasn't so sure. "I don't think he's gotten that bad."

"You didn't expect any of this, correct? Do you have any idea who he really is?"

She thought she did. "So what are you suggesting I do?"

"I'm not saying you have to be dramatic and cause a big fuss. But if you do nothing, you will have no voice in court. You need to hire a lawyer at least. Let him or her do the talking for you."

"I can't afford a lawyer! I have no money!"

"I have a little. I can get you a lawyer."

Tonya's eyes grew wet again. She was so tired of crying. "I don't want to let you do that, Fiona. I'm not sure I'm worth it."

Fiona laughed dryly. "I assure you that your daughter is worth it. This will be hard either way. I went through it and I know. But it's going to be hard whether or not you stand up for yourself. So you might as well stand up for yourself."

"But I don't even want to get divorced!"

Fiona looked shocked. "You can't be serious."

"Divorce is still wrong, despite what he's done."

Fiona looked thoughtful for a moment. "Well, I'm not going to argue about that with a pastor's wife. I'm not saying you have to agree to the divorce. The court will grant it whether you agree or not. I'm just saying you need to make your desires clear. If you want Emma full-time and you want Emma's college savings to be there when she's ready for them, then you need to hire a lawyer."

Chapter 52

Tonya

Emma came out of the bathroom with her hair wet and her face freshly scrubbed. She looked beautiful.

"Are you ready to go church shopping?" Tonya tried to make the prospect sound as exciting as possible.

"We don't really need to go church shopping, do we? Can't we just go to the weird new church because that's where the Puddys go?"

"That's a distinct possibility, but if it's too weird, I might not be able to handle it."

"Deal." Emma rifled through a backpack and came out with her Bible. "But I don't think it's too weird. I trust the Puddys' judgment." She looked at Fiona. "I know you probably don't want to go out, but church is pretty safe. Do you want to go with us?"

Fiona laughed shrilly. "How can you know it's safe if you've never been there?"

"That's an excellent point," Tonya said. "I think most churches are safe, and we're hoping this one follows suit."

"Your last one didn't turn out to be very safe." Fiona's eyes fell. "I'm sorry. That was a little harsh. I don't mean to hurt you two. I've just never had a good experience with any churches."

"Do you have any experience with any churches?" Emma asked.

"Emma!" Tonya scolded. "Let's not pry."

"Truthfully, no, I haven't. But you two are not me, and I am not you. I know we each need different things." She waggled her fingers at the door. "So I'm not going to hold you up. You guys go check it out. I'll be eager to hear how it goes."

Tonya found her shoes and was a little chagrined that she didn't know where her Bible was. Why was her daughter besting her spiritually? "Bye, Fiona." She opened the door and stepped out into the fresh morning air. "Are you sure service starts at ten-thirty?" She didn't want to get there too early and have to endure small talk.

"That's what Mrs. Puddy said."

"I could have sworn those church bells rang at like ten-forty."

"Maybe their clock is wrong." Emma snickered as if she'd said something particularly funny, and Tonya thought maybe she was nervous. Yet she led the way, and she didn't choose to go around the block. She went the same way she had gone when she'd first investigated the church bells, cutting between two lawns and then through someone's back hedge.

Tonya followed her without arguing until they got to the hedge, at which point she started to feel nervous. "I think we should probably take the street on the way back."

"But it's so much farther!"

"That's okay. You're young. You can handle it." The old building came into view. Half of the back wall had now been painted a fresh gleaming white. The place still looked old and a little decrepit, but it gave off a welcoming vibe. She realized she too was nervous. She slipped her hand into Emma's. "Let's hope the Puddys are here already. I feel like I'm going on a first date."

Emma giggled. "I guess we kind of are." She squeezed her mother's hand as they rounded the corner of the building. There were a few cars in the street, but she didn't see either Puddy vehicle.

A woman in a ridiculously giant hat sang out from the front steps. "Good morning! Welcome!" She made a sweeping gesture toward the door.

Tonya would have rather hung out on the lawn and waited for the Puddys, but this woman's persuasive invitation made that difficult. Tonya nodded and smiled at the woman. "Thank you. I'm Tonya, and this is my daughter, Emma."

"Lovely to meet you!" The woman's voice was deep and strong.

Tonya stepped into a small foyer. Before she could lose her nerve, she opened the next door and stepped into the sanctuary.

It took her breath away. Though the building was small, the sanctuary felt spacious and airy. The metal ceiling was gleaming and seemed sky-high. The place felt warm and comforting and smelled like cinnamon. Soft music played, and what looked like brand-new carpet felt soft beneath her feet.

"Why are you crying?" Emma whispered.

Crying? She hadn't realized she'd been crying. She swiped at her tears. "It's just so beautiful," she whispered. "Can you feel that?"

"Feel what?"

Tonya's chest trembled with a silent laugh. "I don't know. But I feel something, and it's wonderful."

Emma rolled her eyes and pulled her mother toward the back pew. "Come on, church junkie."

Tonya let herself be led and then she sat. Emma let go of her hand, and Tonya closed her eyes and let the peace of the place settle over her. She tried to soak it all in. Yes, she was pretty sure that this was their new home. How funny that it was only feet away from their old one.

It was worlds away from their old one. She was a different woman now, living a different life. She heard movement in front of her and grudgingly opened her eyes to see an older woman wearing a contagious smile.

The petite woman stuck out her hand. "Good morning," she said softly. "I'm Esther. Welcome."

Tonya introduced them both again, and they exchanged pleasantries.

"You let us know if there's anything we can do for you. Make yourself at home." Esther gave her another smile and then left her. But within seconds, a new woman stood in front of her.

This woman's face bore years and years' worth of wrinkles, and her mouth was pinched in a painful expression. "I'm Vicky. Welcome." Her voice did not sound one bit welcoming.

Tonya had known dozens, if not hundreds, of Vickys. Apparently, every church had at least one. "I'm Tonya, and this is my daughter, Emma. Lovely to meet you." Fiona's voice piped up in her head, telling her not to fake being pleased at meeting someone unpleasant.

Vicky gasped. "Are you the pastor's wife going through the divorce?" she cried. *Loudly*.

Tonya wanted to die. She wanted the pew to swallow her whole. Maybe this wasn't their new home after all. Maybe if every church had a Vicky, then she wasn't going to be able to go to church.

Esther returned to Vicky's side and tried to pull her away. "Leave them be," Esther said under her breath.

Vicky yanked her arm away from Esther's clutch and leaned against the pew, leveling a gaze at Tonya. "Are you the one? The one who gave us all the dresses?"

Because she didn't know what else to do, Tonya nodded.

Vicky nodded too. "I'm not sure whether to give you my condolences or my congratulations."

Tonya reeled back in surprise. "I'm sorry?"

"I never know what to say to women in your position. Sometimes divorce is a hardship. Sometimes it's God's way of setting women free."

Chapter 53

Tonya

The woman with the crazy hat stepped up to the pulpit and welcomed them all to church. There was only a spattering of attendees, and nearly half of them were Puddys.

Tonya gritted her teeth. She had been so angry with Vicky that she could've slapped her, but her final words had been like a splash of cool water.

Divorce was sometimes God's way of setting someone free? Was that possible? Up to this point she'd thought that God had had nothing to do with any of this. It couldn't have been God's plan for Roy to have an affair. It couldn't be God's plan for her marriage to end. Marriage was sacred. It was till death. She couldn't believe that God had wanted all of this to happen. But maybe God was making the best of a bad situation. Roy had not been a very good husband, and maybe God was setting her free of that. And for the last some-odd years, her heart had not been in the ministry. She'd been doing it for God, sure, but more so, she'd been doing it out of habit. Yet she'd served him fearlessly and faithfully for years. Maybe he was giving her a break. She didn't know.

The woman in the hat introduced herself as Rachel and announced that they did not yet have any musicians so they would be singing their hymns a cappella.

Beside her, Emma groaned. "You've got to be kidding me."

Tonya didn't know if her daughter was disgusted by the use of the word hymns or the lack of an instrument. She thought maybe both.

Tonya stood when she was told to stand, she opened her hymnal to the hymn they announced, and she started to sing the words, but they felt flat. Her heart felt empty. The peace that had greeted her upon her entrance was gone. Now she was just tired, uncomfortable, and wanted to go home. The second song did not help. It was a long dirge she didn't know well, and it went on for eons.

But then the third song started.

"My hope is built on nothing less ..." *Pfft! Hope? What is hope? I have no hope!* "... but wholly lean on Jesus' name ..." *Wait, I haven't been doing that, have I?*

She stopped singing and just listened. Emma looked at her curiously. There weren't very many people there, but they had some strong and beautiful voices. It sounded like far more than a dozen people singing. It sounded like a giant choir was behind her. She focused on their voices. Not only behind her, but all around her. Her chest grew tight, and she clutched the back of the pew in front of her. She squeezed her eyes shut and bowed her head.

Why is this so hard, God? I'm sorry I haven't been leaning on you. I haven't been leaning on anything. "... all other ground is sinking sand ..." *It's so true. I've been standing on other grounds, on marriage, on motherhood, on my church, and I'm sinking, Father. I've been sinking for a long time, but I'm sinking so fast now and I don't know how to stop it.*

A sob erupted out of her, and she tried to keep the noise down. She knew Emma was still watching her.

Please help me to be strong for Emma. I need to be strong for Emma.

"Emma needs to see you leaning on me." The voice came out of nowhere. It wasn't audible, but it was there, inside her head, and it was definitely not her own voice. It was firm but gentle, and she gasped at it.

I'm sorry. I'm so sorry. I'm sorry for everything, for the marriage, for the divorce, for not loving others like you want me to, for being angry at you, for not leaning on you …

Something settled over her then. She felt it on the top of her head, then her shoulders, and then it fell over the rest of her, covering every inch. She knew what it was. She'd felt the same thing when she was six and she'd first asked Jesus to save her. It was forgiveness. It was a clean slate. Tears gushed out of her.

Thank you, Father. Thank you, Jesus. Thank you, thank you …

"In every high and stormy gale," the congregation sang. She stood up straight, shot her arms up into the air, opened her mouth wide, and declared the next line with every part of her being, "My anchor holds within the veil!"

She'd had an anchor since she was six. She didn't know when she'd stopped holding onto it. When life got too busy, or when life got too hard, or when life didn't go the way she'd thought it was supposed to go. At some point, she'd let go, but she was done. She was grabbing hold of that anchor and she was never letting go again. "On Christ the solid rock I stand," she belted out, "all other ground is sinking sand.

"All other ground is sinking sand."

Chapter 54

Emma

Emma climbed into the Puddys' minivan, stepped over the broken seat, and settled into the only empty spot. Everyone greeted her excitedly as if they'd never seen another human before.

She greeted them in return, with slightly less enthusiasm, and then asked, "Where's Victor?"

"Where's Victor?" Peter repeated in a singsongy voice. "Does someone have a crush on Victor?"

Her cheeks grew hot. "Of course not. I was just wondering."

"He had to stay home to help his dad with chores," Mrs. Puddy said. "Peter, zip it."

Peter zipped it.

Mrs. Puddy looked at her in the rearview mirror. "Are you sure your mom doesn't want to come?"

"I tried to talk her into it, but she's busy trying to figure out her life."

Mrs. Puddy laughed. "What does that mean?"

"She's applying for jobs."

"Oh. Did she hear about the secretary position at your school?"

"What?" That would be awesome! She could have her mom right there at school with her? It would only be for one year before she went to high school, but still!

"Yeah, Miss Bennett fell in love with someone on the internet, and she's moving away to marry him."

Peter snickered. "I hope she doesn't get there and find out he's really a fat old man with a pet crocodile."

Mrs. Puddy glared at him in the mirror, and he hung his head.

"Crocodile?" Mary Sue said, giving him a disgusted look. "Really, Peter?" She turned front shaking her head. "I don't know how you come up with this stuff."

Emma pulled out her phone to text her mother about the school job, and every Puddy child leaned toward her to look at her phone. She guessed her phone was pretty exciting to kids who didn't have one. She hurried the text and then hid the phone away. "Thank you for inviting me. I haven't played mini-golf in ages."

"You're welcome. Whether we like it or not, summer is fading fast, so we've got to squeeze in some fun."

"Hey," Judith said, "did you see that all your mom's stuff was gone from the church lawn?"

"Yeah," Peter said. "It didn't even last a few hours. I guess people really like free—"

"So what kind of ice cream is everyone going to get?" Mrs. Puddy said loudly, and Emma shot her a look of gratitude.

Everyone shouted their flavors out.

"What about you, Emma?" Mrs. Puddy asked.

"Not sure. I need to look at the list."

"Ah, a wise woman always considers all her options."

She wasn't sure she was wise, but she loved being called a woman.

The rest of the drive was taken up by the Puddy children arguing about some detail of the Smurf movie they'd all just watched. Emma hadn't seen it, so she was grateful when they pulled into the parking lot of the ice cream scoop.

Mary Sue grabbed her hand and pulled her toward the small wooden building that held the clubs and balls. "We have to hurry, or we'll be stuck with the yellow balls."

Emma laughed. "What's wrong with yellow? I like yellow."

Mary Sue scrunched up her face. "They look all dirty."

They reached the booth, and Mary Sue announced, "Six players, please," as if she was in charge of the whole world.

The teenager towering over them moved his bangs out of his eyes. They immediately fell back into his eyes. "Maximum teams of four."

Mary Sue opened her mouth to argue, but her mother had arrived. "That will be fine. We'll do two teams of three." She smiled at Emma. "The big kids can be on one team, and I'll play with the littles."

Emma beamed. She was a big kid! Mrs. Puddy had a way of making her feel good.

They got their clubs, balls, and score-cards and headed toward hole number one. But then they had to wait. There were a lot of people mini-golfing on a Saturday afternoon.

"So how did you like our new church?" Mary Sue asked while they were waiting.

Emma shrugged. "It was okay, I guess."

Mary Sue looked hurt.

"I liked it," she said quickly. "I'm pretty sure we're going to go there now. My mom *loved* your church."

"What's this about a new church?" a male voice said from behind.

Emma whirled around, prepared to be harassed, but the face behind her was beaming with friendliness. "Oh, hey, Jason."

Jason DeGrave stood before her in all his glory with a blond cheerleader on his arm. Apparently, the scandal wasn't affecting his social life.

"Hey yourself. So you found a new church already? You Christians sure do love your churchgoing."

The girl giggled, but he hadn't meant to poke fun. Emma could tell.

"Church is important," she said and then glared at the cheerleader.

"If you say so. Maybe I'll come check it out sometime. Hey, sorry to hear about your house. That stinks."

Her cheeks got hot. "How did you know about that?"

He laughed. "Are you serious? Because your dad showed up at my mom's house with a bunch of furniture."

Emma's stomach plunged toward the ground.

Jason's smile faded. "I'm sorry. I thought you knew."

Mary Sue inched closer to her.

"He's moved into your house?" She knew she'd spoken the words, but her voice didn't sound like her own.

Jason laughed angrily. "It's not my house. Me and my dad left. But yeah, he's living at my old house. Again, sorry. I didn't mean to tell you weird news in a joking way."

"That's okay. I'm glad to know it."

They stood there for an awkward moment, and then Jason said, "Well, it was great to see you. I feel like we've been through a war together or something." He forced a laugh. "I'll see you around." He nodded toward the first golf hole, which was now open.

"Yeah, I'll see you around." She tried to smile, and then turned away.

"See you around the golf course," Mary Sue mumbled. "They're going to be following us around for the next hour."

"Nah, they'll be following your mom around. We'll be much faster than them."

Mary Sue giggled and stepped up to the green. She placed her ball and then swung the club like a pro, but the ball didn't travel like a pro ball, and Emma laughed. Mary Sue laughed too. "Let's see you do better!"

She didn't know if she could. She put the ball down, hoped Jason wasn't watching, and then gave it a whack. It traveled straight and true, but stopped shy of the hole. She went to stand beside Mary Sue while her brother took his turn.

"Mary Sue?"

"Yeah?"

"Should I tell my mom?"

Chapter 55

Tonya

Emma shot through the door like a puppy who'd just been let out of his crate.

"I take it you had fun?" Tonya asked, smiling.

"I did! And now I've got a sugar high!" She giggled and held up a fluorescent green card. "I won, so I got a free game! Wanna go play another round?"

Tonya leaned back from Fiona's laptop and stretched her back. "How did you win? You never play mini-golf."

Emma took an exaggerated bow. "I guess I am just a natural." She plopped down in a chair on the other side of the table. "Or Mary Sue and her brother were really bad. Did you get my text?"

She nodded. "I did. Are you sure you want me to apply for that? I would be at school with you. I don't know if you want me so close all the time. I don't want to cramp your style." She said it in a joking tone, but it was a serious concern.

"Are you kidding? I would *love* to have you there all the time! Please, please, apply for the job! Please!"

Her heart soared at Emma's response. What a great kid she had. "Okay, okay, I will, but applying doesn't mean I will get hired."

"You will!"

Fiona came into the room nodding. "I think you've got a good chance. You've got the right skill set."

"What skill set is that?"

She opened the fridge. "Smiling at people you don't want to smile at and running the show without getting any credit." She pulled out a can of soda and popped it open, looking self-satisfied.

"All right. I'll print out another resume."

Emma looked confused. "Mrs. Patterson has a printer?"

"No, I've been going to the office supply store. They print them for me for a small fortune. This will be my third trip today."

"Your mother also hired a lawyer!" Fiona said proudly. "She's a ball of fire today."

Tonya laughed. Fiona might have been kidding, but any kind of praise felt good.

Emma shifted in her seat uncomfortably.

"What is it?" Had she changed her mind already?

Emma didn't immediately respond.

"What is it, Emma?" Her mind was racing to dark places.

"Dad's moved in with Mrs. DeGrave," she spat out.

Tonya leaned back in her chair and exhaled. "Oh, is that all?"

Fiona cackled in delight. "That's my girl!"

"Is that all?" Emma repeated, incredulous. "I thought you'd be horrified!"

Tonya thought about it. "I guess I'm horrified in a detached, objective sort of way. But I'm not really any more horrified than I was yesterday." She smiled, trying to comfort her daughter. "I think I've maxed out on horror."

Emma still looked stunned.

"Your mom is becoming strong." Fiona held up one arm as if flexing her bicep and then shook the whole arm in the air. "She is too tough to be hurt anymore! She is pulling herself up by her bootstraps!"

Emma's shocked expression morphed into one of confusion.

"*I'm* not really doing anything," Tonya said quickly. "But God is doing a lot." She reached across the table and took Emma's hand. "I'm still hurt, of course, and I'm still praying that God fixes all this somehow. But I'm not nearly as hurt as I was. And I'm not scared anymore. I know God has us."

"Good," Emma said.

"How did you find out?"

"Jason was at the golf course."

"Ohh," Fiona cooed. "The great Jason plays miniature golf?"

Emma ignored the bait. "Print out another resume and then start praying that he gets you that school job. Then I won't have to ride the bus!"

Tonya laughed. So *that's* why her daughter wanted her at her school. Emma had been complaining about the bus ride for ages. They'd built the school miles outside of town, so it wasn't a quick ride. And it was a ride full of bullying, foul language, bad smells, and mean pranks.

She'd begged her to drive her to school, but Tonya had usually been too busy. "I will pray for this job, and I will pray that if I don't get this job, God will give us a way to get you to school without riding the stinky school bus."

"I'd offer to give you a ride, but my car won't start," Fiona said, and they all laughed.

Chapter 56

Esther

A t New Beginnings Church, there was a small room beneath the steeple. They'd taken to calling it "the upper room," and that's where the seven ladies were gathered on Sunday morning at ten, praying over the service.

Esther heard the smoke detector first. She didn't panic, though, as it went off every time one of them used the toaster. "Someone should probably go check on that."

"I'll go," Vera said, and Esther almost laughed. Precious Vera moved like a snail.

"No, it's okay. I'll go." Esther beat her to the top of the stairs and started down. She was halfway down the stairs when she smelled smoke, and she let out a little screech as she picked up speed.

They'd put a few appliances in the back corner of the sanctuary, sort of like a makeshift kitchen, and that's where the smoke was coming from. And there was lots of it. A frying pan sat on top of the stove, and the flames it contained were a foot high. Coughing, she looked around for something to smother the fire with. One of Rachel's hats lay nearby, and while it was big enough, she wasn't sure Rachel would ever forgive her. She grabbed a cutting board off a nearby table and slammed it down on the fire, silently praying that it would do the trick. It did.

"What's going on?" Vicky cried from the bottom of the stairs.

"Where are the pot holders?" Esther cried.

"We don't have any! What's burning?"

Esther ripped off her cardigan, wrapped it around her hands, and then grabbed the handle of the still-smoking pan. She could feel the heat through the sweater. "Someone open the doors!" she cried and saw Rachel heading that way with Barbara on her heels.

Esther rushed out through the doorway and down the steps. Her hand was burning now, so she flung the mess, sweater and all, onto the lawn. Then she looked at her hand to access the damage. None was visible, but it still hurt. She turned to go up the steps.

"You can't just leave that there," Vicky said.

"I'll get it when it cools off. I need to go run my hand under cool water."

"I'm so sorry!" Rachel cried. "I totally forgot!"

"What were you doing at the stove?" Cathy asked. They didn't usually let Rachel near the stove.

"Dawn was going to make her homemade doughnuts, and she asked me to start the oil."

"I didn't tell you to start it on high!" Dawn cried, turning the burner off.

"I'm so sorry," Rachel said again.

Esther shoved her hand under the cold water. "It's fine, Rachel." She looked over her shoulder. "It really is. No harm done, and we've got a great story."

"Great story?" Vicky cried. "We've got people coming in a few minutes, and this place is full of smoke!"

"And I've got no pan for the doughnuts!"

Esther turned the water off and turned to face her teammates. "Open all the windows. I'll run next door and grab my fans. Barbara, can you go get some doughnuts from the coffee shop?"

Barbara nodded and turned to go.

Vera appeared at the bottom of the stairs. She squinted at them. "Is it smoky in here?"

No one answered her but instead started running around to the windows. Esther hurried next door, but she was just about out of energy, so her hurry wasn't very fast.

She grabbed her bedroom fan and her living room fan and then left her apartment, suddenly aware of how heavy fans were. She was grateful for the elevator, but then it was a long trek down the street.

Roderick Puddy met her in the driveway. "Let me get those for you!"

Vicky met her on the steps.

"How is it in there?" Esther asked, panting.

"Better than you'd think since we almost burned the place down."

"The bells," Esther said, out of breath.

"What?" Vicky cried.

"I haven't heard the bells."

"Oh, beans! Now the bells are late again." She reached out and grabbed a Puddy child by the collar of his shirt. Then she hollered, "Rachel!"

Rachel appeared.

"Go teach this child how to ring the bells. Then it can be his job from now on."

The child beamed.

Esther started to walk by Vicky and go inside, but Vicky grabbed her arm. "I'm thinking of doing something that I know is absolutely insane."

Well, *this* sounded interesting. "What?"

Vicky bit her lip. "But I think God wants me to do it."

"Do what?"

Vicky looked at her. "Would you help me?"

"Help you do *what*? I don't know if I want to help you to do something that's absolutely insane."

"Come on." Vicky went inside, and with reservations, Esther followed. Vicky marched right up to Tonya and Emma and said, "You know that giant yellow farm right beside the school?"

Tonya, looking terrified, nodded.

"Well, that's mine. And it's a big place. I'm having trouble keeping it up. I was wondering if you two would like to move in with me, for free, and help me keep the place going."

Tonya's mouth fell open.

Emma's whole body started shaking with excitement. She grabbed her mom's arm with both hands. "Mom! It's right beside the school!"

"I'm a little forgetful these days. I need help with things. Nothing major, just stuff you need to do to keep from dying in your own house."

Tonya's mouth moved, but it took a few seconds for words to come out. "Thank you for your generous offer. Can we pray about it and get back to you?"

Vicky gave her a curt nod. "I wouldn't have it any other way." Then she turned and went to the front.

Esther followed her and sat beside her. "My friend, I think you just did a *very* smart thing. I don't think that was insane at all."

"We'll see."

Chapter 57

Fiona

Fiona watched them walk to the end of her driveway and turn right. Despite Emma's proclivity for cutting across people's backyards, Tonya had put her foot down. They were going to take the street, like civilized folks.

Soon they were out of sight, and Fiona missed them. She couldn't believe, after years of being content to be alone, how quickly she had grown attached to these two women. They felt like family. She knew they wouldn't be with her forever, and she dreaded the day her house would be quiet again.

She had almost been tempted to accompany them to church, but they hadn't asked. They'd assumed she wasn't interested, and she was grateful for that. But the temptation had still been there. She was intrigued by this new little weird church they'd found, though she didn't know if she should think of an old crumbling down church as new. New or old, it didn't sound like other churches. For starters, it was apparently founded and run by her peers. She couldn't imagine taking on such an endeavor at her stage in life and she admired the women who did. She thought they were nuts, but she admired them.

She pulled herself away from the window, settled into her comfy armchair, and picked up the remote control to spend some time with some fictional friends. She scrolled through the shows, looking for something comedic.

Tonya and Emma rejoined her four episodes later and they were glowing. They were so bubbly they were verging on irritating.

"I take it that it went well?"

"The ladies tried to make homemade doughnuts," Emma said with a giggle, "and almost burned the church down."

"Homemade doughnuts are tricky," Fiona said, feeling a bit defensive. "I'm impressed they even tried."

"It was very kind of them to try," Tonya said. "And even when the experiment failed, they still managed to find doughnuts. But never mind that. Something far more exciting than a fire happened!"

Fiona raised an eyebrow. "Oh? What could be more exciting than a doughnut fire?"

"A woman named Vicky ... I don't even know her full name, but anyway, Vicky apparently lives in the giant yellow farmhouse right beside Emma's school and she lives there all alone, and she is struggling. So she invited us to come live with her. We would help out around the house, and she would let us live there."

It was a knife to Fiona's stomach, but she tried to hide it. The expression on Tonya's face suggested that she had failed to hide anything.

"Fiona," Tonya said. "You can't imagine how grateful we are. I don't know how we would've gotten this far without you. You've been so good to my daughter and then to me. We will never stop being grateful and we don't plan to lose touch with you. But this house is small, and I know you value your space. And I think this woman genuinely needs our help. But that doesn't mean we're leaving you." She looked at her daughter, who nodded her agreement. Then she looked back to her. "You can't get rid of us now."

Fiona tried to find her voice. "Right beside the school, huh?"

Tonya nodded. "I don't have the job yet, but it just feels like everything's coming together, like God has a plan, and all the puzzle pieces are snapping together."

Fiona looked down at her hands. If God had plans, they never included her, and she was about to watch some of her puzzle pieces walk away.

Chapter 58

Emma

Emma slept in on Monday morning but when she got up, Mrs. Patterson was still in her pajamas. She hadn't seen Mrs. Patterson in her fancy silky PJs since that first night when Emma had woken her after midnight. Why was she in her pajamas now? Was she not feeling well?

"Good morning," Emma said.

Mrs. Patterson was in her chair, staring at the television, her left hand clutching the remote and her right hand wrapped around a glass filled with one of her iced coffee brandy concoctions. "Morning," she said without looking at Emma.

"Did you have breakfast yet?"

Still not looking away from the TV, she shook her head.

"Want me to fix you something?"

"No thank you," she said tonelessly. "Not hungry."

This was strange on so many levels. Mrs. Patterson wasn't being rude but she wasn't being her normal feisty and funny self either.

She found her mother in the kitchen working on Mrs. Patterson's laptop. "What are you doing?"

"Looking for more jobs."

Emma's chest tightened. "Why, did you hear from the school?"

"No," her mother said quickly. "But it's still good to have a plan B. And a plan C. And maybe a plan Z." She smiled. "You hungry? I can fix you something."

Emma nodded. "Yeah, that would be great."

Her mother stood up and went to the fridge.

"Is Mrs. Patterson okay?" Emma whispered.

Her mother held one finger to her lips. "Careful. She has eagle ears. I don't know. I tried to talk to her earlier, but she's not in a talking mood. I think we should try to give her space but be close enough so she can have us if she needs us."

Emma disagreed wholeheartedly. "I'll be right back." She went back into the living room. "The ladies at church are having a tea party tomorrow morning."

Mrs. Patterson laughed derisively.

"I was wondering if you would like to go?"

Mrs. Patterson looked at her dryly. "You don't need to worry about me, dear. I appreciate you caring, but you don't need to find me friends. I don't need friends, and I don't want them." She turned her red eyes back to the television.

"But I think you'd like them. They're funny and spunky and, even though they can be a little rude sometimes, they are always entertaining."

"I said no!" she snapped, and there was something in her eyes that Emma hadn't seen before. It wasn't kindness.

"I'm sorry," Emma mumbled and then quickly left the room.

Tonya gave her a soothing smile. "It was a good idea, honey," she whispered. She pulled her toward the corner of the kitchen, far from the living room. "Mrs. Patterson's issues go even deeper than we understand. I don't think there's going to be a simple solution. We just need to keep loving her and keep praying for her. If God wants her out of the house, he will make it happen. If God wants her to have new friends, he will make that happen too."

Emma shrugged. "Maybe."

"He got her to open the door for you, didn't he?"

Chapter 59

Tonya

Emma had gone for a walk, and Tonya strongly sensed that Fiona wanted her out of her house as well. "I'm going to step out for a little bit. You need anything from the outside world?"

There was a long hesitation before Fiona answered her, and Tonya wondered if she'd even heard her. "No thank you. You have a good time." Had that been sarcasm? Tonya wasn't sure. She stepped outside, not sure where she was going—but then she saw the church steeple and decided to go pray. She wasn't sure the church would be unlocked, but she had a feeling.

She could hear the ladies bickering before she'd even crossed the lawn. Did they live there? She stepped inside and was greeted by paint fumes. Esther, Vicky, Cathy, and Dawn were all there.

She coughed. "You want me to open some windows?"

"Well, hello there!" An enthusiastic voice called from above.

Tonya looked up to see that Rachel was on a ladder. Was that safe? No one was spotting her. Tonya hurried to the ladder. "Do you need some help?"

"That is not a good question to ask around here," Esther called from across the room. "I suspect we will be needing help around the clock for at least the next six months." She started across the room carrying a paint pan and a brush.

Tonya took them from her. "Oh, shoot, I kind of like this shirt. Not sure I should paint in it."

"That's the second time I've wished we hadn't thrown out those old choir robes."

"When was the first time?" Rachel called down.

"When I needed something to put out your fire!"

Tonya laughed.

"What brings you here?" Esther said. "Everything all right?"

"Yes. I came to pray."

Esther swept an arm toward the altar. "Well, don't let us stop you!"

"That's okay. I can pray and hold a ladder at the same time." She took a long breath. "Do you know Fiona Patterson by any chance?"

Esther shook her head. "I don't think so."

"Well, she's my friend. She lives on the next street over, and she's had a rough go of it. But despite her own issues, she has taken my daughter and me in, and—"

Esther's eyebrows flew up. "Does that mean you won't be accepting Vicky's invitation?"

She looked so disappointed that Tonya rushed to say, "No, it doesn't mean that. Fiona's house is very small, and we don't really fit. And I've applied for the secretary position at the school, so living with Vicky might be perfect. I'm sort of waiting to hear about that job before I make any final decisions."

Esther's face relaxed in relief. "Oh good. So how can we help this friend of yours?"

"She's something of a recluse. Part of me can support that, but part of me knows she needs others in her life. She's made it clear she's not interested in Jesus, but I sure would like her to meet him, as well as you ladies."

The rest of the ladies pretended they weren't eavesdropping, but they had all stopped painting and were holding perfectly still.

"Would you guys pray for her for me? That she develops the desire for God, but that she also lets other people into her life? I feel like her coming to visit here would take care of both things, but I've learned lately to let God make the plans."

Esther laughed. "Let's pray right now." She stepped back and held her arms out to her sides. "Come on, ladies. Let's get this done for Tonya. And for Fiona."

The others assembled around her in a small circle. Tonya hung back at first, but then Esther beckoned her into the circle. Rachel took Tonya's right hand, and Cathy took her left.

"Father in heaven," Esther began. "We ask for your interference in Fiona's life. I don't know her, and yet I know that you love her. Please make that love impossible to ignore and impossible to resist. Please shower her with a desire to find out more about you and your love. Please bring her to us so that we can show her your love. Please give her a seeker's heart and tell us how to best minister to her. In Jesus' name we pray. Amen."

Everyone echoed, "Amen."

Tonya looked up with tears in her eyes. "Thank you."

Esther nodded. "That's what we were put here to do. Keep us posted and let us know if we can do anything."

"This morning my daughter invited her to your tea tomorrow, but she declined. With a bit of snark."

Esther closed her eyes again. "Father in heaven! PS! Please bring her to ladies' tea. That's a great idea! In Jesus' name we pray again. Amen."

"Amen," the women echoed for the second time.

They started to scatter back to their paintbrushes, but then Esther cleared her throat. "Father in heaven," she said loudly.

The women all stopped moving and closed their eyes.

"PS again! Could you also please land Tonya the job at the school? In Jesus' name we pray! Amen."

"Amen!"

Tonya smiled at Esther. "Thank you. I can't believe how much I want that job."

"That probably means God's put the desire in your heart." Esther turned to go back to work.

Tonya looked at the ladder and then looked at Rachel. "Hey, you want me to take a shift up top?"

"Don't I ever!"

Tonya expertly ascended the ladder. She had built more Vacation Bible School sets then she could count. She dipped Rachel's brush into the paint and got to work, taking care not to drip anything on her shirt. "This is a lovely color you ladies picked out."

"It was on sale. How goes the divorce?"

The question startled Tonya. She still had trouble with the word divorce. It wasn't a word she associated with herself or her circumstances. She still didn't want to get divorced and had been praying mightily against it. "I'm not sure. We have a magistrate date, so I guess that's the next step. But I don't plan to fight him for anything. We don't really have anything to fight over. I'm just going to ask him to leave Emma alone."

"Is he her father?"

"Yes, and of course he can still be in her life," Tonya hurried to say, "but I don't want her out of my life. I don't want her spending weeks and weeks with him when I can't be with her."

Rachel was quiet.

"I know it sounds selfish, but trust me, it's not. I want what's best for Emma, and right now, that's being with her mother."

"I support you fully," Rachel said, sounding sincere. "And I'll be praying about your meeting."

Chapter 60

Fiona

They sounded like a flock of guinea hens coming up her walk. Without moving the curtain, lest they see it and be encouraged to approach, Fiona eyed them at an angle. Seven of them. They looked about her age, but some of them were moving quite well. Only one had a cane. One of them carried a pie.

What was it with these Christians and their pies? Was that in the Bible somewhere? Was there a pie commandment?

One of them tapped softly on her door.

"Is someone at the door?" Emma called from the couch.

"No! And hush!"

Emma came to stand beside her. "Who is it?" she whispered.

"I'm assuming it's your church friends. They have pie."

"Oh!" She stepped toward the door, but Fiona caught her arm. "Don't you dare!"

Emma looked at her with wide, innocent eyes. "What?"

"You told them about me and you brought them here, but I will not let you encourage this further by opening the door!"

"Oh, for Pete's sake!" an unpleasant voice came from outside. "You've got to knock louder than that!" Someone pounded.

"You'll break the door, Vicky!"

"I didn't tell them about you!" Emma whispered.

Fiona looked around. "Where's your mother?"

"I don't know. I just woke up."

It was true. She had just woken up, though it was past eleven.

"I'm guessing she's in the backyard."

This was probably also true. Tonya had been spending a lot of time in the backyard lately, reading her Bible. Fiona didn't understand how anyone could read the same book over and over again.

"Let's go," one of the women said. "She's probably not going to answer."

"Are we sure she's home?"

"Tonya said she's always home."

Aha! So it *was* Tonya who had ratted her out!

"All right, well, set the pie down."

"Set it down where?"

"Right there!"

"Critters will get to it!"

"Well, what are you going to do, carry it back to the church?"

Emma looked at her imploringly. "Please let me open the door."

"No! It's not worth it!"

"Put the pie down now!"

"Fine."

There was a scuffling, and then, "But don't cry to me if some stray cat gets into the pie." Her voice faded as she spoke.

"Cats don't eat pie!"

"Stray cats will eat anything..."

Fiona could still hear them, but she couldn't make out what they were saying. She pulled the curtain back. "I'll be darned."

"What?"

"They're taking your shortcut." She let the curtain fall shut. "Go ahead. Go get the pie."

Emma hurried to the door.

"But don't you dare call to them!"

Emma did as she was told, and soon there was yet another pie on Fiona's kitchen table. "It's still warm." Emma looked up at her. "Pie for breakfast?"

"Breakfast? It's lunchtime! And yes, pie for lunch. Why don't you go ask your mother if she wants some? I'll find the slicer."

Emma went through the back door and returned within seconds with her mother in tow. Tonya clutched a giant worn Bible.

Fiona tried to hide how annoying this was. She didn't know why it bothered her that the woman was suddenly obsessed with the ancient myth-filled book, but it did. And Tonya was acting differently too. Fiona didn't know if it was because of all the Bible-reading. She realized Tonya was watching her and forced a smile. "Pie?"

"I hear the entire church brought you a pie?"

Fiona nodded. "A whole gaggle of 'em."

Tonya chuckled. "I'm sorry I missed them."

Fiona wasn't. She might not have been able to stop Tonya from opening the door. And then where would she be? Trapped in her own house with a kitchen full of guinea hens.

"You okay?" Tonya asked, her brow worried.

"Absolutely." She sliced into the pie, and her mouth watered. She might be annoyed that those women came to her door, but that didn't mean she had to let homemade pie go to waste. "Looks like strawberry rhubarb. That's great news." She slid the first slice over to Emma, who had settled in at the table. "You might want some milk to go with it." She glanced up at Tonya. "Unless you'd rather have tea?"

"Great idea. I'll make some." She went to the stove while Fiona cut her a slice and then another for herself.

She sat down and started in. It was, as she'd anticipated, heavenly.

"You know, Fiona," Tonya started.

Here it comes.

"I think you'd really like some of those women. They're pretty spunky."

She tried to focus on how good her pie was, but it was suddenly less pleasurable.

"Maybe you'd come to church with us, just once? We could flank you on either side, protect you."

Fiona dropped her fork. "I can protect myself, thank you."

"Of course you can," Tonya said quickly. "I didn't mean to suggest you couldn't. I just wanted you to know we'd have your back." Her phone rang and she reached for her pocket. The tea kettle started to whistle, but she ignored it. "Hello?"

Fiona felt sorry for the person on the other end of the line, having to contend with that whistle.

Tonya listened carefully, said, "Yes, yes, absolutely, okay, and thank you," and then hung up. She looked at Fiona and Emma with wide eyes. "That was the school. I have an interview."

Fiona pushed her plate away. She'd lost her appetite.

Chapter 61

Fiona

On Saturday morning, someone pounded on Fiona's front door. What was going on? She takes in a few homeless Christians and suddenly she lives in Grand Central Station? She remembered her time spent in Grand Central and shuddered.

Tonya was headed for the door.

"What are you doing?"

She paused. "I'm going to answer the door."

That's what she'd been afraid of. "Please don't."

"It's Roy."

Fiona stopped. She didn't know what to say or do.

Tonya went the rest of the way to the door and then hesitated. She squeezed her eyes shut, took a long breath, and then opened the door and smiled genially.

Why was she smiling? What was she up to? Fiona stepped closer to get a better view.

"I'm sorry, I can't invite you in. It's not my house." She tittered nervously.

He didn't look at her face but seemed focused on her knees instead. "That's okay. I don't need much time. I need you to sign this health care paperwork." He shoved a manila envelope at her. "They won't remove you from the policy without your permission."

She took the envelope. "I'll sign it right away. How should I get it back to you?"

His face twisted up into a hideous expression. "Can't you just mail it? Do I need to buy you a stamp?"

Somehow, Tonya's smile didn't waver. What was wrong with her? "Of course, I'll mail it. I didn't realize that would be all right. And what about Emma?"

He still wouldn't look at her. "What about her?"

Still smiling. These people weren't even acting human. He was acting subhuman. She was acting superhuman.

"She's on the policy too. Are you keeping her?"

"I'm dissolving the entire policy. I'm not keeping anyone."

"Oh."

They stood there for a few seconds, and then he started to turn away.

"Wait."

He half-turned back. "What?" Was there something physically wrong with this man's eyes that prevented him from looking at his wife? Now that Fiona had had the thought, he didn't look well. He was awfully pale for August, and he looked weak and thin. By contrast, Tonya was tan from all her backyard Bible-reading, and she looked hearty as a horse.

"The magistrate meeting, what—"

"We're not supposed to talk about that. That's why we have a magistrate."

Fiona didn't think that was true.

"I know, but I want to make this easier on you."

He flinched, and his eyes came up to her waist. "What?"

"What do you want, Roy?" Her voice had softened, but that odd supernatural smile was still there.

"I want a divorce."

She nodded. "And?"

"And nothing." He sighed, and his expression turned a bit more human. "I want to be free of my old life and free to live a new one."

"And Emma?"

The humanness vanished. "I don't really want to be discussing this on some weirdo's porch."

Fiona grimaced. That's what one gets for eavesdropping.

"I'm trying to be agreeable. What do you want for custody?"

He shrugged and turned his head to gaze off into the distance. "I would still like to see my daughter."

"Good. And are you asking for any particular amount of time?"

He shook his head. "Maybe just a dinner now and then."

Tonya's body visibly relaxed. "And her college fund?"

Finally, he looked at her. His head snapped toward her, and he snarled. "So that's what this is all about? You're after the money?"

She laughed. "It's not that much, Roy. I'm not after it for myself. It's for Emma's college. I want to make sure it stays—"

"It's gone."

Her body froze. "Gone?"

"That's what I said." He started to walk away.

"My lawyer will be quite interested to hear that—"

He turned back. "You hired a *lawyer?*"

"Let me finish!" she said firmly. "But I won't raise a stink as long as you leave the custody of Emma to me. You can still see her, of course, but she'll be living with me."

He appeared to be considering that. "Fine."

She smiled again. "Thank you. And ... I'm sorry, Roy."

He jerked.

"I'm sorry I wasn't a better wife."

He staggered back a step, and when he spoke, his voice had lost all anger. "You were a good wife, Tonya." Then he turned to go, and it was evident that nothing his wife could say would stop him.

Tonya closed the door, turned, and leaned against it. She exhaled deeply. "Well, that was unexpected."

"What is up with you?"

She stood up straight and laid the paperwork on the table. "What do you mean?"

"I mean, why didn't you claw his eyes out and then kick him where it counts?"

Tonya giggled. "I thought about it."

Fiona doubted that.

"But I've spent a lot of time listening to God about this situation, and I think what I've heard is that I can't control his behavior. I can only, by the power of the Holy Spirit, try to control mine. So it is my job to be gentle and meek and to turn the other cheek."

Fiona snorted. "You rhymed."

Tonya giggled. "Yes, I suppose I did."

"So you're not mad at him? Not even a little?"

Tonya looked contemplative. "I don't know. I'm disappointed. I'm still sad. But no, I don't really feel angry with him anymore. Mostly all I feel is peace about the whole thing."

"That is so very bizarre."

Tonya laughed. "Welcome to the Kingdom of God, where most things are."

Chapter 62

Fiona

Fiona had no intention of going to church with the Mendell women, even though she'd come to decide that Jesus was indeed having some weird supernatural effect on Tonya. That's the only explanation Fiona could come up with as to why Tonya was okay. It had taken Fiona more than a year to stop sobbing over her divorce, and hers hadn't even been as messy as Tonya's. As public, yes, but there'd been no big church or daughter in the mix.

Yet, when Emma invited her at the last minute, she couldn't quite get her mouth to form the word no. Emma stopped moving and stared at her, her young face filled with an almost obnoxious hope.

Fiona didn't want to disappoint her. But she didn't want to go to church, either.

Or did she?

Part of her was mightily curious about whatever transformation was taking place in Tonya.

Emma rushed toward her and hugged her from the side. "Oh please, oh please, oh please!"

Fiona tried to pull Emma's arm down from her shoulders, but she only tightened her grip. Fiona looked at Tonya. "You'll stay on either side of me?"

She nodded resolutely. "Absolutely!"

What was happening? What was she doing? And why was she doing it? "I'll have to get dressed."

The church bells started to ring.

"You look perfect the way you are," Tonya assured her.

Fiona realized then that both Tonya and Emma were wearing jeans. So she would be better dressed than them, at least. "Should I dress down?" She'd meant it as a joke, but her voice was shaky.

"No. Don't change at all. Come just the way you are. That's the way Jesus likes it." Tonya came alongside her and looped an arm through hers. Emma relaxed her hug then and took her other arm.

"Now I feel like I'm being arrested."

Emma giggled. "Have you ever been arrested?"

"Of course not! Who do you think I am?"

Emma picked her Bible up off the table. "I don't know. You're some kind of a rock star from what I understand." She started to pull her toward the door.

Despite herself, Fiona laughed. *Rock star.* Indeed.

Suddenly, they were out in the sunshine, and Fiona's feet stopped moving. They felt like lead blocks on the ends of her legs. She was partly relieved by their decision and partly embarrassed. "I'm sorry."

Both women stopped pulling. The tenderness in Tonya's eyes turned Fiona's heart to mush.

"Don't be sorry," Tonya said gently. "I understand."

"You do?" How?

She nodded. "More than you know. But I also know that you are going to feel better if you keep walking. Whether or not you decide to fall in love with Jesus today, you will feel better if you walk forward than you will if you turn around and play it safe."

She snickered. Fall in love with Jesus? This woman had really been sniffing the Bible glue. She told her feet to move, and surprise of all surprises, one of them did. She almost gasped.

"There you go," Tonya said, her encouragement one hundred percent sincere, without a hint of condescension.

And then Fiona's other foot came alongside the first, and then she was walking again. Like a normal person. "You can let go of me now."

They hesitated.

"And I think we should take the shortcut. It will give me less time to change my mind."

The closer she grew to the big white building, the stronger her panic grew. What was she doing? How had she let these two Jesus freaks get into her head? She needed to turn around. Right now!

But she didn't. They rounded the corner of the building, and Emma gasped.

"What?" Fiona asked, alarmed.

"The sign!"

Sure enough, right in front of them was a giant wooden sign. It looked hand-painted. Beautiful calligraphy read, New Beginnings Church. "Is that new?"

"Yes," Tonya said. "All of this is."

"Yoo-hoo!" someone called from ahead, and Fiona looked up to see a woman in a ridiculous hat. She looked familiar, and Fiona assumed it was one of the pie-delivering guinea hens.

"That's the one who started the doughnut fire," Emma whispered, and Fiona let out an inappropriately loud cackle.

Maybe she was something of a guinea hen herself.

"Is this Fiona?"

"Yes," Tonya said.

"Well, welcome!" The woman seemed genuinely thrilled at the sight of her. This woman must not get out much either. "Come on in and make yourself at home."

Unlikely.

With a friend on either side of her, Fiona went up the steps and then inside. Her panic was so thick she could hardly think.

And then she saw it.

It looked like more than forty pipes—three ranks of them—stretching to the ceiling. They were a beautiful silver that looked so sharp against the oak that it took her breath away.

"You okay?" Tonya asked.

She realized she had stopped walking. "Yes," she said breathily. Then she started again, straight for the organ. It was calling to her in a way that made her eyes water. Why was such a magnificent instrument trapped in a falling-down building?

She slipped off her shoes and then slid onto the bench. It felt like home. She heard the congregation fall silent behind her and grew self-conscious. She turned around, and Emma was right there behind her.

"Sorry," Fiona said. "I shouldn't have presumed. It's just so beautiful." She turned back to the console. "I wanted to see it up close."

"That's cool. Nobody minds."

Her fingers hovered over the bottom manual. "Do they have an organist?"

"No, we don't have any musicians."

Fiona closed her eyes and let her fingers fall. They played a few notes from a lifetime ago and then stopped.

"Don't stop!" one of the guinea hens cried.

Tears slid down her cheek as she pushed in some of the stops. Then she started again, and her whole body, her whole being, sank into the melody as her fingers danced across the keys. Her feet found the pedals, and she was off. She thought she had forgotten.

But her body remembered. Her heart remembered.

Tears gushed out of her. She knew people were listening. She knew they would critique her and criticize her.

She didn't care.

The organ was out of tune.

She didn't care.

This organ needed to be played, and she knew she'd been brought there to play it. All these years, it had been so close, but it had sat all alone. All these years the musician and the instrument had been within shouting distance, but walls had kept them hidden from each other.

Not anymore.

She started a second song and let her mind go with the music. She didn't think about anything. She let her soul ride the melody as years of pent-up art flowed out of her. All she could feel was the music. All she could hear was the music. The technically trained young woman inside of her knew that her old rusty fingers were making mistakes, but she couldn't hear a single one of them.

She finished the second song and realized the sanctuary was still silent. Had everyone left? She stopped and turned to look, and a man sitting in the middle of the sanctuary jumped to his feet and started applauding.

Oh no. She had an audience.

She hadn't wanted that.

Her chest tightened in shyness and panic.

But Emma was right there and placed a warm hand on her back. "It's okay. You're safe here. This is God's house."

Others followed the man's lead, and soon everyone in the building was on their feet. She didn't know what to do. She took Emma's hand to steady herself and then got to her feet. "Let's go sit down. I didn't mean to make such a spectacle of myself."

"Spectacle?" Emma cried. "That was a gift! A huge gift to all of us! Thank you!"

She gave her young friend a sincere smile and allowed herself to be led to a pew.

Chapter 63

Fiona

The crazy-hat lady stepped up to the pulpit and made a bunch of announcements, but Fiona had trouble focusing on them. Her whole body trembled. How good it had been to play again! Maybe she could ask the guinea hens if she could come here and play sometimes, when no one was there. She couldn't believe she'd given an impromptu concert, but she hadn't been able to help herself. It was as if some supernatural force had pulled her to the building, then to the bench. And how glorious it had been! She felt a little self-conscious, but it was impossible to regret what had just happened.

The hat lady told them all to greet one another, and Fiona groaned. *Oh no.*

"That's weird," Emma said. "They never do this. There are only like twenty of us, and we've already greeted each other."

"I think I know why," Tonya said, but she didn't elaborate.

Suddenly, the hat lady was standing right in front of Fiona. "Absolutely no pressure," she said, holding up two white-gloved hands. "We usually sing a few hymns now, and we usually do it a capella, because we don't have a piano player." She hesitated. "Again, no pressure, but would you be interested in playing the hymns for us?"

Fiona froze. How had she not seen this coming? "Uh ..."

"I don't think she's up for that," Emma tried, but Tonya shushed her.

"Let Mrs. Patterson decide. I think she might surprise you."

Tonya was right. What was happening in Fiona's head right then was surprising even her. She nodded. "Sure." She couldn't believe it, but her body *wanted* to play the hymns.

"Do you read music?" the woman asked.

Fiona snorted. "I can read music with my eyes closed."

"She went to Juilliard," Emma explained, sounding amusingly proud.

"Oh good. We have hymnals, but I know some people play by ear. Hard to do that with a song you don't know." She tittered. "Come back to your organ, Fiona." She started to walk away, and Fiona followed her, leaving her safety net of friends behind. The woman looked at her. "You can't even imagine how blessed we are to have you here today. We've been praying for you."

This admission stunned and terrified Fiona, and she stopped walking. She stopped breathing.

The woman read her body language perfectly. "Don't be scared off by that. If God only sent you for one day, then we'll enjoy that one day. As I said, absolutely no pressure. And I mean it. God wants people doing things because they want to, not because some crazy lady pushed them into it." She cackled.

Fiona forced a smile and started walking again. Soon she was back on the bench with an ancient hymnal in front of her. The cover was sun-faded, and the edges were threadbare. She tried to imagine how many hands had held the book, how many lips had sung the words.

"Thank you again," her escort said. "You are a miracle."

No one had ever called her a miracle before. A prodigy, yes. Gifted, yes. Talented, of course. But never a miracle. At first she didn't like the idea. It seemed to give God the credit for all the hard work she'd done.

Then she looked down at her gnarled fingers. She'd worked hard, yes. Incredibly hard in those early years. But if God was real, then he'd given her those fingers. And if God was real, he'd given her her ear. And when she was almost mummified by loneliness and immobility, he'd sent her friends.

Her *soul* had been immobile. Frozen. Dead.

And now it felt like she was coming back to life.

She'd never heard the first song they sang, but the congregation was sure fired up about it. They kept shouting, "Victory!" and though she couldn't see them, she imagined they each had one fist shot into the air.

The next song was much calmer, and the words washed over her like a gentle ocean wave: "As I come so weak and weary ..." She was the epitome of weary. "All my life is sad and dreary; let me enter by the door." The door? What door? Should she be trying to find this door? This thought scared her, and she focused on the melody instead of the lyrics.

But then the next song started, and these lyrics were impossible to ignore: "Softly and tenderly Jesus is calling ... see on the portals he's waiting and watching ..." These Christians were as obsessed with doors as they were with pies. But it was the chorus that made her throat swell shut. The melody alone was mesmerizing. Even without the lyrics, it beckoned to her, made her feel wanted and loved. And the words pushed her over the edge: "Come home, come home. Ye who are weary, come home."

She almost stopped playing but willed her fingers and feet to keep going.

Come home. What a concept. She'd already been home. She'd already been safe within her walls. What home was this song talking about? It crossed her mind that the song meant heaven, but she didn't think these people would be inviting one another to die. So that meant there was another home, one she didn't know about, and she could feel someone calling her there.

The woman with the hat spoke above the music. "I believe there is someone here today who wants to come home."

Fiona's breath caught, and her chest tightened in panic. She kept her eyes on the music and hoped against hope no one was looking at her.

"If it's you, come on down so we can help."

There was a rustling, and Fiona fought the urge to look. Someone was going down front, and it wasn't her, thank goodness.

No one sang, but she kept on playing, as she hadn't been told not to. The mood in the place had shifted, and she followed accordingly, softening the music and taking liberty with grace notes. She was being blessed by her own music. How long it had been!

Whatever was happening at the front of the church went on and on, and eventually, Fiona sneaked a peek. A young man stood in front of the hat lady. His shoulders shook with his tears. The man who had originally stood to clap for her was there with a hand on the younger man's back. All the heads were bowed—

Wait. Was that the DeGrave boy? What on earth was he doing here? And why was he in the front of the church making a spectacle of himself? Fiona turned to look at Emma, and she was crying too.

These Christians were an emotional bunch.

She turned back to her music, trying to dismiss their behavior as unfounded emotional fervor—but the lyrics wouldn't leave her mind alone. *Come home, come home. Ye who are weary, come home.*

Chapter 64

Tonya

Tonya thought maybe she was going to be sick. She glanced around the hallway for a restroom but didn't see any. If her stomach betrayed her, she would have to run out into the parking lot. She squeezed her eyes shut and prayed this wouldn't happen. She was wearing Fiona's shoes, and she didn't want to soil them.

At only thirty seconds past the hour, they called her name. She stood, straightened her skirt, and tried to display a confidence she in no way felt as she walked into the principal's office. The principal greeted her warmly but professionally and then introduced her to the school's other secretary, whom she might be working alongside. This woman was notably less warm and less professional in her greeting, but Tonya tried not to care.

The principal motioned to a hard metal chair and then sat down.

She followed suit.

"So, Tonya, tell us about yourself."

She inhaled and then froze. *Words, Tonya. You're going to have to use words.* "Well, I've been helping to run a church for over a decade. It had a lot of moving parts, and I learned to be organized but also adaptable. I work well with other people, and ..." She wasn't sure where to go next. "And I'm good at appearing civil and professional, even when I'm not civil and professional on the inside."

The principal laughed heartily. The other secretary didn't. Tonya assumed that she was *not* good at faking professionalism or civility.

"I'll be honest," he said, "your reference letters are convincing. I think you'd be great for this job. But I should warn you. Sometimes the students are not pleasant. How would you handle blatant disrespect?"

Her first thought was of her husband, but she thought she'd leave him out of it. She smiled. "I used to go out into the street to share the Gospel. I've heard every mean word in the book. I've been threatened, I've been chased ... I've even been spit on."

His eyes grew wide, and she wondered if she'd said too much. Maybe he didn't want an evangelist in the school office. She opened her mouth to promise him that she wouldn't be proselytizing any of the students, but he didn't give her a chance to speak.

"Are you good with computers?"

"Efficient. I've done lots with PowerPoint, Excel, and Word. I'm no IT specialist, but I can find my way around."

He smiled, studying her. "What do you think you might struggle with in this position?"

She didn't know. She hadn't thought about that. "My daughter will be in school here. It might be hard for me not to follow her around."

She hadn't meant it as a joke, but he tipped his head back and laughed at the ceiling. Then he stood, stuck his hand out, and said, "I like you. Welcome aboard."

Stunned, she accepted his handshake and then turned to the other secretary, who forced a smile. Tonya initiated a handshake with her as well, which she weakly accepted.

Tonya couldn't get back to Fiona's fast enough. She couldn't wait to tell Emma.

Emma didn't even need to ask. She could read it on her face. "They gave you the job?"

Tonya nodded wildly. "They did! Let's celebrate!"

Fiona came into the kitchen. "Well, I'll be. I thought maybe they'd hold the church drama against you."

Tonya smirked. "Thanks for not telling me that before."

Fiona laughed. "I would never! But, congratulations, sincerely. I'm glad they saw you for who you really are."

"He mentioned my letters of reference." A few of the women from church who wouldn't speak to her had jumped at the chance to write her a letter. Tonya had seen no harm in putting their guilty consciences to good use.

Fiona rolled her eyes. "Good. I'm glad those came in handy."

Tonya slipped off her shoes. "And the shoes. Thank you. I'm pretty sure that's what gave me the competitive edge."

Fiona laughed. "Keep 'em. I haven't worn them in years."

"But won't you want to wear them to church now?" Emma said, and Tonya flashed her a look that said, *Don't push.*

"I have plenty of shoes. Your mother is going to need some school clothes because she gave away all her dress clothes."

"That's okay. I'm looking forward to some thrift store treasure hunting. I want to look more professional and less like an eighties pastor's wife. I feel like I'm being reinvented."

"You are," Fiona said. "God's getting you ready for the next chapter of your life."

Tonya *loved* to hear Fiona crediting God with something, but she tried not to let the excitement show. Didn't want to scare her away.

"So I suppose this means you'll be taking that cranky Vicky up on her offer?"

Tonya nodded. "But! Seeing how cranky she is, we would really appreciate being able to come visit here often."

Fiona nodded slowly. "I suppose that would be all right. But don't bring friends."

Emma went to Fiona and wrapped her arms around her. Fiona visibly stiffened beneath the embrace. Tonya realized her daughter was crying. "I don't know how to ever thank you."

Fiona patted her arm. "You don't need to thank me, dear."

Emma let go of her and stepped back.

"I should probably be thanking you. If you hadn't been crying on the lawn, I never would have invited you in, never would have gotten to know the awesome person that is you." She looked at Tonya. "And then I never would have met your mother." She took a long breath. "I was alone, and I'm not alone anymore." She laughed and held up both hands. "I'm not saying I'm ready for a social life. I still think people are mean and rotten, and I don't want much to do with them, but you two have shown me that not everyone will hurt me. Maybe having one or two people in my life is a good thing."

"Definitely," Tonya said.

"Does that mean you'll go to church with us again?" Emma said hopefully.

Fiona shrugged. "Probably. I don't know who else is going to play that pipe organ."

Chapter 65

Emma

The first soccer practice of the pre-season wouldn't start for another twenty minutes, but most of the girls were already there, excited and anxious. They sat on the bleachers or stood in front of them, chatting nervously. Isabelle was regaling them all with tales of her exclusive soccer camp, where she'd learned how to do a flip-throw. Emma was completely certain that this was a lie and that Isabelle would never attempt a flip-throw in front of them.

She saw Jason DeGrave coming from a distance. She turned to look behind her, wondering where he was headed, but there was nothing behind her but trees. She turned back and watched him come. She hadn't seen him since he'd gone down front at church, but she'd been praying for him ever since.

He waved in her direction, and she almost turned to see if there was a cheerleader behind her. She gave a tentative wave in return, and then he beckoned her over. She realized that most of the girls had stopped talking. They were watching the exchange. Nervously, Emma stood and brushed off the seat of her shorts, gaining some satisfaction from the fact that Isabelle's mouth was hanging open.

She walked over to Jason, trying to look cool. "What's up?"

He looked over her shoulder at the rest of the junior high girls. "You realize they're all staring at us?"

She grinned. "You're quite the spectacle."

He laughed, and his dimples were wonderful. "Hey, I was thinking." He looked sheepish all of a sudden. What could he possibly be feeling nervous about with her? "I've been trying to read my Bible, and it's so hard. And there's really no pastor to call." He laughed, and she imagined how much he didn't want to call Rachel or Esther. "I've looked for some answers online, but I'm only getting more confused. Anyway, I was thinking maybe you and I could do some Bible study, but then I thought that might be weird with just the two of us, so I was wondering if you knew anyone else who might want to join us. Thought maybe we could have a before-school Bible study once a week or something."

She wasn't sure how to react.

"Feel free to tell me that's a terrible idea."

"No, no," she said quickly. "I think it's a great idea. I'm not sure how much help I'm going to be. I only recently started really getting into the Bible myself, but we can certainly try. And I might be able to find someone else to join us." She was thinking of Mary Sue, which was a little weird because she didn't even go to school. "Probably be junior highers, though."

He grinned. "That's okay. My friend will probably join us too, but he doesn't know any more than I know."

"Okay, then. I think it's a great idea. I actually live right in that big yellow house." She pointed at Vicky's farm. "Do you guys just want to come over there? I'll try to get my mom to make muffins or something."

He looked relieved. "Yes, that would be awesome." He looked over her shoulder. "I still can't believe all this Jesus stuff is real, you know?"

She nodded, even though she didn't really understand. She could never remember a time when she didn't know Jesus was real.

"I wouldn't believe it myself, but *something* called me into that church, and when I got in there, I realized it was him. And he's been calling to me ever since. I've never felt such purpose, you know?"

She nodded again.

He grinned broadly. "All right then. How about Monday morning? Get us ready for the week?"

"Sounds good."

He looked over her shoulder again. "They are all still staring at us." He gave her a scheming look. "Emma?"

"Yeah?"

"I am a junior and you are an eighth-grader, so I promise I'm not hitting on you."

She froze. What was happening?

"And we might be stepbrother and stepsister soon anyway."

She shuddered.

"But I think it would be super funny if I kissed you on the cheek right now."

At first she didn't understand. Then she remembered that Isabelle's eyes were firing daggers at her back right now. She grinned. "Actually, I would really appreciate that."

He laughed, and then, before she was even ready for it, he wrapped his arms around her in a real hug. He spun her a little to give her teammates the best view and then he planted a big kiss on her cheek.

She thought maybe her knees would melt, but they didn't. It only felt like a friend's kiss on the cheek. And that was okay. He stepped back, winked at her, and said, "See you Monday at seven?"

She nodded. "Make it six-thirty. And thanks, Jason."

He looked surprised. "For what?"

"For ruining Isabelle Martin's day."

He laughed, and she turned to rejoin her team. Her heart was pricked by the knowledge that the Jesus in her wouldn't want her to rejoice in Isabelle's horror, but she still allowed herself to do it. Just for a minute.

Epilogue

Tonya

Nervously, Tonya stepped behind the pulpit. "Thank you, Rachel, for leading the singing, and thank you, Fiona, for that beautiful music." She cleared her throat. "And thank you all for singing. You sounded like a choir of angels." She smoothed out the already smooth paper in front of her. "As you all know, I am not a pastor. Not even close. But Cathy asked me to share my testimony today, and God has made it clear to me that I should never argue with Cathy."

A polite laugh rippled through the small congregation.

"I am so sad to share that my divorce became final this week." She let out a long breath. That had been easier to say than she'd thought it would be. "I never thought I would be a divorced woman, and sometimes that still feels like a huge failure." She shrugged. "Maybe it is. Either way, God has not given up on me.

"I never wanted to be in a difficult marriage. I never wanted to be betrayed by my husband. And I never wanted to be a divorced woman. But I'm not as regretful about all of that as you might think.

"You see, I was a busy pastor's wife. I was serving God fifteen hours a day, seven days a week, but I hardly knew him. I was simply going through the motions. I didn't know it at the time, but I didn't try to spend time with God, I didn't spend much time talking to him—except when I was late getting somewhere and I didn't have enough gas. And I didn't ever thank him for anything. I was too busy, always out of breath." Her voice cracked, and she swallowed.

"Looking back, I don't even recognize myself. When things fell apart, I prayed that God would put them back together. And he hasn't done that in the way that I would've planned. Some people might look at me and think that he hasn't put it back together at all, but they would be wrong.

"I am closer to God than I have ever been. I have such peace and such joy. And my daughter is closer to God than she has ever been." She looked at Jason DeGrave, sitting beside Emma. "And others have come to fall in love with Jesus because of the messiness I've been through.

"So here's what I want to tell you. If things don't seem like they're going right in your life, that might be a good thing. They might not be going your way. You might be going through horrible, embarrassing things that you didn't think were supposed to happen. And maybe they weren't supposed to happen. But that doesn't mean that God isn't going to use them, and it doesn't mean that you're not going to be okay.

"I know for a fact that the opposite is true. You *are* going to be okay. Because we don't need our jobs or our reputations or our homes or even our marriages to be whole. We just need God."

She smiled broadly. "We just need God."

Books by Robin Merrill

New Beginnings
Knocking
Kicking
Searching
Knitting
Working
Splitting

Greater Life
Forgive and Remember
A Good Day to Live
No Time to Win
Bridge to the Present
A Good Man Is Hard to Lose
Picture Imperfect

Piercehaven Trilogy
Piercehaven
Windmills
Trespass

Shelter Trilogy
Shelter
Daniel
Revival

Printed in the USA
CPSIA information can be obtained
at www.ICGtesting.com
LVHW051222101223
766132LV00011B/897